"Every baby is a girl."

"Are you sure they're all mine?" Alex asked, incredulous his wife had accomplished such a feat.

"They're all tagged Banning, sir."

"You didn't accidentally grab up too many?"

"No, they're all Daphne's."

Alex looked back at his progeny. One tiny bundle squirmed in her blanket wrappings, starting a chain reaction. Suddenly, all three pairs of eyes were open and staring around. Alex closed his eyes. A whole new, unexplored world laid out its vastness before him. Lace and ruffles. Diaries and separate phone lines. *Boyfriends...* Oh, Lord. *Three* girls.

And if they were anything like their mother, they'd have their daddy wrapped about their pretty pink fingers inside of five minutes.

Dear Reader,

Don your white dress for three special occasions—
a christening, a debutante ball and a wedding!
Three favorite American Romance authors prove
that "No one can resist a woman in white!"

Tina Leonard leads off the series with the most
lovable rugged cowboy daddy you've ever met!
And be sure to catch Vivian Leiber next month
with *Secret Daddy* and a special presentation by
Anne Stuart in March, with *The Right Man*.

Happy reading!

Debra Matteucci
Senior Editor & Editorial Coordinator
Harlequin Books
300 East 42nd Street
New York, NY 10017

Daddy's Little Darlings

TINA LEONARD

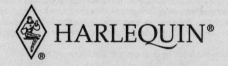

TORONTO • NEW YORK • LONDON
AMSTERDAM • PARIS • SYDNEY • HAMBURG
STOCKHOLM • ATHENS • TOKYO • MILAN • MADRID
PRAGUE • WARSAW • BUDAPEST • AUCKLAND

ISBN 0-373-16758-X

DADDY'S LITTLE DARLINGS

Copyright © 1999 by Tina Leonard.

All rights reserved. Except for use in any review, the reproduction or
utilization of this work in whole or in part in any form by any electronic,
mechanical or other means, now known or hereafter invented, including
xerography, photocopying and recording, or in any information storage
or retrieval system, is forbidden without the written permission of the
publisher, Harlequin Enterprises Limited, 225 Duncan Mill Road,
Don Mills, Ontario, Canada M3B 3K9.

All characters in this book have no existence outside the imagination of
the author and have no relation whatsoever to anyone bearing the same
name or names. They are not even distantly inspired by any individual
known or unknown to the author, and all incidents are pure invention.

This edition published by arrangement with Harlequin Books S.A.

® and TM are trademarks of the publisher. Trademarks indicated with
® are registered in the United States Patent and Trademark Office, the
Canadian Trade Marks Office and in other countries.

Printed in U.S.A.

Prologue

"Good morning, gentlemen! Keep that stiff upper lip, Alexander Number One," Daphne Way Banning sang out as she hurried past the six somber portraits of the Banning Boors. Hanging in the great hall of the Green Forks Ranch, the portraits lent austerity and a sense of family continuity to the Banning mansion. Privately, Daphne thought that the portraits needed more than a good dusting. They watched her with grim lines where their mouths should be and eyes that seemed disapproving and cold.

Wait until they hear my news, Daphne thought excitedly, *it'll really send those stiff lips to their noses.* "Where's Alex, Sinclair?"

"In with his father, Miss Daphne." The elderly valet looked her way. "I don't think Alexander is feeling very well this morning."

"Oh, dear." Daphne hurried along. She had some news that might please the ailing Alexander. The patriarch of the family, he had let it be known since the moment Daphne and Alex had gotten back from the honeymoon that he expected to see grandbabies. Soon. They had been very careful not to oblige him too quickly, not out of a sense of meanness but simply from needing time to get to know each other as husband and wife. Oh, she'd been in love with Alex Banning forever, long before he'd known she was alive on the neighboring ranch. He had been slower to give his heart. She'd been surprised when he proposed after a three-month-long whirlwind courtship, packed with trips to Europe and yacht outings and heady romance. Daphne had said, "Yes! Yes!" when he asked for her hand. A dream come true...

She wondered how Alex would feel about her news. They had been so careful not to get pregnant, but temptation had proved too great one enchanted Saturday night. Wild kisses sometime after midnight turned into a burning urge to get home and finish what they had started. Running upstairs and getting into bed, they'd spent hours passionately loving each other. The box of condoms lay undisturbed in the bedside table drawer.

Too late to worry about that. Daphne walked to the bedroom, which had become a sickroom, and listened for voices to make certain Alexander was awake. She didn't want to disturb him if he was resting.

"Promise me, son."

She heard her husband sigh. "Dad, I don't have to promise. Everything will turn out fine."

"I don't have much longer to live. I want to know before I die that you understand you must produce a son!"

"Fine, Dad. But if you don't mind, we're going to wait a while before we work on it."

"It's been three months! What are you waiting for?"

Daphne stood still, but she heard Alex's footsteps on the opposite side of the room. They were rapid and impatient, as if he'd gotten up from the bedside to stare out the window.

"We barely know each other, Dad. I know this dynasty thing is big on your mind, but right now, Daphne and I aren't thinking about producing heirs."

Wrong, husband. We are now—in about six months, Daphne thought unhappily. She touched her stomach protectively.

"Son, let me tell you a story."

"Hopefully one I haven't heard before?"

Daphne started to smile.

"Sit down!" Alexander thundered.

The smile froze and then slid off her face. She heard her husband sigh again as he sat down.

"For six generations, there's been one male child born into each Banning marriage. Who knows why? I've often wondered if it was a curse left over from the days when our forefathers were bravely beating pagan enemies off the English shores. One child, and no more," Alexander rasped.

"One's enough. We didn't need an heir and a spare."

"Take it seriously, Alex. What if there hadn't been an heir each time?"

There was quiet in the room for a moment. "Tell me, Dad."

"Females would be running the ranch! Wives who married into the family! It would slip out of Banning hands, and may I add those hands have capably handled the reins ever since our forebears came over from England!''

''Don't get excited, Dad. It isn't good for your blood pressure. And Green Forks isn't a kingdom.''

Daphne heard Alex sigh once more.

''In England, we'd by damn be aristocracy! It's important that we retain our illustrious heritage! Two governors, a couple of corporate CEOs, a successful wildcatter and a world-renowned chef. Greatness must carry on!''

Coughing erupted in the sickroom, and Daphne started to hurry forward in alarm. Alex's next words stopped her cold.

''It's a mistake to have children when you're not sure if the marriage is going to work out.''

Her jaw dropped. She backed up, her hand tight against her heart.

''Son, I know you didn't want an arranged marriage. I know you feel like I pushed you into marrying that girl.'' Alexander took a deep, racking breath. ''But think of what it was like every time I drove past their pitiful, broken-down ranch. Always another son popping out of Mrs. Way. A girl, of course, the time she had triplets, but still sons in the mix. Damn if I didn't start wondering if it was secret water Cos Way was pumping up out of an underground well just to spite me. Hates me, he does, and I hated him. I swear he kept that woman pregnant just to show me what a real man could achieve. Six sons, every one of them strapping and healthy and tall as live oaks.'' He took a deep breath. ''No, I know you didn't like me arranging the marriage, but I had to do it. You understand, don't you?''

Daphne's heart froze in her chest. She waited forever for her husband's reply.

''I do, Dad. Go to sleep now. Everything is going to be all right.''

Tears welled in Daphne's eyes as cold shock spread through her. Everything was *not* going to be all right. She backed up quietly and hurried downstairs, wiping at the tears running down her face. *When he said he liked my jeans, I should have known he meant genes,* she thought wildly, running past the Banning Boors, still watching her coldly and aristocratically. She felt like turning the portraits to the wall, but it wouldn't help. Nothing could help her.

Her husband had been forced to marry her.

Chapter One

Five months later

"We have located her, sir."

The valet's stiff voice held a ring of achievement, of a job done well. Alex Banning held in a sigh of relief. His heart sped up at the thought of finally seeing his wife again. "Good. Bring her, and our baby, to the mansion."

"She's very weak, but she is resisting us, sir."

"Of course she is," Alex said matter-of-factly. "Have you ever known Daphne Way to ever do the conventional thing? To go along quietly because someone asks her to?"

Sinclair chuckled. "No, sir."

"Well, then! Do what you have to. Negotiate. But bring her here. And the baby," he added as an afterthought.

"Yes, sir." The car phone was disconnected.

Alone in his mansion, his nerves on edge, Alex waited for the woman who had borne his child to be brought, probably kicking and screaming, to him. Months ago Daphne had run from their marriage.

He'd nearly gone mad when she left, with only a short note telling him she wasn't coming back. Though he'd gone several times to her parents' house, they had said little except that she didn't want to see him. His heart broke. His greatest fear was realized. They *had* married too quickly without allowing her time to get used to living in the Banning mansion. Without time to really get to know her husband. And when she had, she hadn't wanted him.

Through a friend, he discovered she was pregnant. Realizing that Daphne had no intention of contacting him, he had sought her at the school where she taught.

She had responded by showing him the door. Then she quit her job and moved from her parents' home. Her new phone number was unlisted.

The worst blow had been the delivery of divorce papers. A hundred knives had gone through him when he read them.

He'd retreated. He kept his eye on her through various means, none of them obvious enough to alert her to his knowledge of the baby growing inside her. Knowing Daphne, she'd leave the country, and then he'd have to go through serious maneuvers to keep in touch with her.

He'd kept quiet until the birth, though it nearly killed him. The thought that the woman he loved was bearing his child without him by her side was enough to drive him to complete insanity. There had been a complication, but he didn't know what. Nurses went to the small apartment once a day, Sinclair reported, and Daphne went to the hospital much earlier than the due date Alex had circled on his calendar. It had been what he thought would be several months into her pregnancy, but since he had no idea when she'd gotten pregnant, he had no idea how far along the baby had been. *Dear heaven, let it be healthy. Let Daphne be fine.* He called the hospital, but they would give no information on her condition or the child's.

Alex had been left with nothing to do but worry himself ill.

Today, Daphne had finally left the hospital. He had dispatched Sinclair at once.

Daphne Way was going to live in the enormous mansion in Green Forks, Texas, with him, whether she liked it or not. This place was big enough for the both of them and one tiny baby.

"I HAD NELLY take Miss Daphne—Mrs. Banning—upstairs," Sinclair informed Alex when he arrived thirty minutes later.

Alex hovered in the marbled hallway, as nervous as if he'd been in the delivery room himself. Which he should have been, but there was nothing he could do about that now. "Is she all right?"

"Miss Daphne is weak, but not weak enough to forgo giving me a tongue-lashing. She doesn't want to see you, sir."

"I know. Where is my son?"

Sinclair looked at him oddly. "In the library."

Alex grimaced. "I would have been down sooner, but I got caught on an overseas phone call."

"Of course, sir. I will show you to your, er, child."

Alex followed Sinclair into the library-turned-nursery, his hands trembling. He was a father! In time, another oil painting could be hung in the great hall alongside the other portraits of Banning men of great accomplishments. His own son.

He stopped in his tracks at the sight of three little blankets spread across the floor with a tiny baby securely wrapped on each. There was a flurry of activity as servants pulled baby things from boxes and bags.

"What is going on?" Alex demanded. "What are those?" He pointed to the baby bundles. "Why are they lying on the floor?"

"We weren't prepared for three." Sinclair shrugged. "We only bought one crib and one set of baby accoutrements."

A sinking sensation hit Alex. Perhaps an error had been made and the Banning mansion had been mistaken for an orphanage. "Those are not all mine, are they?"

"I'm afraid so. Trust Miss Daphne to do the ever-flamboyant thing."

"Oh, my God." Alex couldn't believe what he was hearing. "Are you sure?"

"They're all tagged Banning, sir."

"You didn't accidentally grab up too many?"

"No, sir. They are all Daphne's babies."

Daphne Way was a hell of a woman, but he didn't think she'd been capable of *that*.

"In poker it's called a three of a kind, sir. Very advantageous. Congratulations."

Alex ignored the felicitations and moved forward to eye the sleeping bundles. "Have you called for extra everything?"

"Yes."

"Daphne didn't require extra hospitalization?" He whirled to glance at Sinclair.

"No, but as I said, she is weak. In spite of your questionable methods, sir, I believe this is the best place for her."

"Yes." Alex blinked at the first bit of criticism Sinclair had ever leveled at him. He looked at his progeny. One tiny bundle squirmed in its blanket wrappings, starting a chain reaction. Suddenly, all three pairs of eyes were open and staring around. "What are their names?"

Sinclair stepped close to examine the baby on the left. "That one, I believe, Miss Daphne called Yoda."

"Yoda! She named my son after a fictitious intergalactic creature?" His roar set Yoda to crying and the help to a standstill. After an astonished second, a nanny came forward to pick up the child and comfort it with a malevolent glance at Alex.

"I don't know her proper given name, sir. That's all I heard Miss Daphne call the child."

"Well." That would have to be fixed, though Alex could see how the triangular-shaped head and big dark eyes might have earned the baby the nickname. Suddenly, his brain processed what his ears had heard. "*Her* proper given name?"

"Yes, sir. Miss Daphne has done you the honor of giving you three daughters."

"I—" There were only Banning male portraits hanging in the great hall. "Every single one?"

"Every baby is a girl."

He closed his eyes. A whole new, unexplored world laid out its vastness before him. Lace and ruffles. Diaries and separate phone lines. *Three* girls. He'd better buy stock in the phone company.

Boyfriends.

Oh, Lord. "And this one?" he demanded, pointing to the next baby on a blanket.

"That one is Miss Magoo."

"Miss Magoo!"

"Mr. Magoo if it had been a boy, of course. You see the resemblance."

Alex stared at the lashless baby. She grinned hugely at him, unaffected by her surroundings. With the big bald head, he supposed the baby did resemble Mr. Magoo. With luck, she'd grow hair eventually.

In trepidation, he looked at the smallest baby. It was by far the most unattractive creature he had ever seen. To Alex's mind, this wizened child had a face only its mother could love. "What did this homely child's unnatural mother name *her?*"

"I believe Miss Daphne affectionately called her Alex Junior. Alexis, in the feminine sense, I should think."

"This is the one she chose to bear *my* name?" Astounded, he stared at the tiny baby, who appeared to glare back at him. Daphne's eyes, Daphne's mouth and no doubt Daphne's temper. "She's scrawnier than the others. And, though I hate to say it, she's...ugly."

"Sir, please. The child hears you."

"Well, her mother will soon hear me, as well. Something's got to be done about these names." He reached down, gently picking up Alex Junior. "This one doesn't look like me at all. Why do you suppose she named this one Alex Junior?"

"She said that one was forced out of the um, chute, sir. Miss Daphne commented that being forced to do something against its will was in keeping with your situation." Sinclair coughed delicately, but Alex knew he was trying to laugh. "She was the first child born. I believe it is customary that firstborn males bear their father's name. Miss Daphne believes gender shouldn't affect any situation adversely."

It damn well did. Alex stared at the baby doubtfully, receiving the full force of haunting Daphne eyes watching him. He sighed, almost frightened by the morning's events. If Daphne did anything by convention it would be a first, and Sinclair knew it. He handed the baby to the valet with a shrug. "I'm going to see Daphne now."

"I would take an heirloom from the vault, sir."

Alex paused, thunderstruck. "An heirloom?"

Sinclair kept his head turned stiffly forward. "It is generally looked upon favorably by the mother to receive a token from the father of her child, signifying his appreciation for her propagating his lineage."

Alex's brows raised. "Are you suggesting a tiara?" Did three babies require more of an appropriate gesture than one baby?

"Your mother's pearls should do nicely, though I do believe Miss Daphne isn't in a relenting mood."

"I'll stop by the vault on my way to her room." Alex's chest tightened as he left the nursery. If he owned a diamond mine in South Africa and signed it over in her name, Daphne would likely not care.

He wondered if she had ever loved him—the way he'd loved her.

Still loved her.

Chapter Two

Alex walked into the large bedroom he and Daphne had once shared. His heart thudded uncomfortably as he looked for the woman who'd sent him divorce papers. Receiving them had nearly killed him. He'd wanted to shred them and throw them into a fireplace, but he'd filed them away in a cabinet. He couldn't put her off forever. If she insisted on the divorce, he guessed he'd have to give it to her. It would be a hell of a one-year anniversary gift, one he didn't want.

"Daphne? Are you in here?" he asked softly, glancing around the room.

She popped her head out from inside a closet. His heart stopped instantly, and his mouth dried out. Daphne was the most beautiful woman he'd ever seen. Not pop-culture beautiful, no. Classically beautiful, with beautiful, large green eyes. Bronze hair waved down over her shoulders.

"Alex." She came from the closet and seemed to find it hard to look at him.

"I—I brought you this," he said stiffly, holding out the velvet pouch that contained his mother's pearls.

She shook her head. "I don't want anything from you."

He bit the inside of his jaw, wondering how to proceed. What should he say to this woman who'd just borne his children? "You look beautiful," he said honestly.

"Thank you."

Her voice was gentle and quiet—and somehow unconvinced. Alex scratched his neck and cleared his throat. "I saw the babies."

"Oh?" She briefly met his gaze before finding a place on the floor to stare at.

"I'm a bit overwhelmed to find myself a father of three all at once." He smiled to show her he was taking it well, but she kept her vision trained to the ground. "How are you? Being a mother of three...I can't imagine what you've gone through," he said helplessly.

"I'm fine." Shrugging, she went back to sorting baby things. "Managing."

"Is there any way I can help?" He really, really wanted to help her in any way she needed.

"Not pulling commando tactics on me would be nice. Just because you have half the world's money doesn't give you the right to drag me and the babies away from our home." She stared at him belligerently.

He spread his hands in front of him, struggling to understand the hidden meaning behind her words. The tiny apartment she'd leased didn't seem to be much of a home to him. Their home was here, at Green Forks, if he could only convince her of that. "You belong here, Daphne, no matter what our relationship is.''

''Even divorced? You would want me here?''

Swallowing tightly, he said, ''Of course. Those are my children. You are my wife.''

Her eyes were wide. ''Even if I'm not your wife?''

He couldn't bear to think about it. As long as he could put it off, he wasn't signing those papers. Daphne had married him for better or worse, and by heaven, he had to convince her that being his wife fell under the heading of better. ''Let's not talk about that right now.''

''We have to, Alex! We have to talk. You may not like to, but we probably should have done more talking before we got married.'' She sank into a chair. ''I'm so tired. Can we argue some other time?''

Instantly alarmed, he said, ''I'll call Nelly.''

''What for? I want to rest, not have to talk to one more person.''

Sudden tapping in the hall electrified her nerves. It sounded like a cane. It sounded like—

''Daphne. You're back.'' Aided by Sinclair, Alexander walked into the room.

She bristled at the tone in his voice, which seemed to imply that she'd returned of her own free will. She was amazed by the recovery he'd made. He looked like his old self again. ''For the moment,'' she said with a lift of her chin.

''Hmph.'' He leaned on his cane. ''Like your mama, birthing triplets. Where's the boy?''

''Sorry to disappoint you, but apparently that's one

way I'm not like my mother.'' She glanced at Alex purposefully.

"They're beautiful girls," Alex said. "Didn't you think, Dad?''

"Hmph. Ugly names. Yoda. Miss Magoo. I do think you could give them proper names, Daphne." He turned to stump out of the bedroom before turning his grizzled head to glance over his shoulder. "It's not your fault, of course. It's my boy who seems to be chock-full of feminine chromosomes."

Daphne sucked in her breath and quickly glanced at Alex to see how he took his father's criticism. To her surprise, he laughed out loud.

"See you at dinner, Dad," he called.

"Didn't he hurt your feelings?" Daphne still cringed from the visit.

"Absolutely not. Dad may be fixated on boys, but the minute he found out you were pregnant, he made a recovery even the doctors couldn't believe. You gave him three grandchildren, Daphne," he said huskily, "and he'll consider them an honor."

"What a good liar you are." Daphne moved away. "He's made no bones about the fact that only boys will do for him."

"True. But he'll have to get over his hierarchical delusions." He stood, preparing to leave the room. Daphne did look tired, and he wanted her to rest. "There could be other children, anyway, Daphne, not that it's something either one of us want to think about right now."

"No. There can't be." She folded her arms, suddenly chilled.

"I mean, once we've talked about this divorce thing," he said hastily. The last thing he wanted her to think was that he was patronizing her. "I don't want a divorce. I want to have a hand in raising my children. It's best if we stay married."

Her insides felt like cement. "I can't have any more children." Guiltily, she looked at Alex.

His mouth fell open. "What?"

Sadly, she shook her head. "The doctor says I can't."

"Why not? Your mother had eight."

It was impossible not to see the fear and disappointment in her husband's eyes. Daphne knew she might as well lay all her cards on the table. Alex had a right to know. "I'm not sure what happened. It all went so fast! There were nurses and doctors and babies crying and tubes—" She shivered, stepping away from Alex when he held his arms out to her. "All I know is that, the next morning, when the doctor came in to see me, he said that I had a rare disorder where the uterus prolapses. He felt it would be dangerous to my health to have more children."

"I see." All the blood leached from Alex's normally tan skin.

Daphne's heart dropped into her shoes. "Now you see that the divorce is necessary."

"No, I don't." He shook his head slowly. "I'm sorry you had to go through all of that alone."

"What about not having a son?"

He shrugged. "It's not the end of the world."

"Your father will be unhappy."

"I don't live my life to make my father happy."

True, Daphne conceded. But he had made a promise to the old man, which at the time had been a deathbed vow. His father would still want a Banning heir. And she knew how bad he wanted it.

Bad enough to buy all her father's cattle at top prices during a drought. Alexander Senior and her father had called it a business arrangement. It had really been a dowry.

"You might not live your life to make your father happy," she said softly, "but he lives because he thinks you're going to give him what he wants. And to be honest, it's a huge strain to live under, Alex. I don't mind staying here for a week or two until I get a little stronger, but then I want to go back to my apartment. I hope you'll understand."

"Our anniversary's coming up," he reminded her. "One year of marriage. We can't throw that away, even if it hasn't been conventional, especially now that there are children involved."

She shook her head. "I'm sorry. There's just too much in our way. I'd like to celebrate our anniversary by finalizing our divorce."

"Very well. If I can't change your mind." His face appeared carved from stone. "However, I think you should factor in a compromise, since I'm prepared to give you the divorce you want."

Daphne was instantly wary. If he asked her to leave her babies behind, she would refuse. "What?"

"Since it's two weeks until our anniversary, I suggest that you allow me that time to see you and the babies and to do my best to change your mind about a divorce."

"I won't." Her blood raced as she thought about Alex trying to change her mind. He was a handsome man, tall and distinguished. Dark, well-trimmed hair and black eyebrows, which were fixed in a scowl right now. Such blue, blue eyes…and a good heart. That's what she loved the most about him. He was a good man through and through. When he said something, he meant it. She admired that—even when he'd made the promise to his father. But she couldn't withstand two weeks of him trying to change her mind. Because she would, especially in her weakened condition. She wanted to right now….

"You say you won't, but I think for the babies' sakes, we should give our marriage a second chance." He ran a hand through his hair, ruffling it so it sprayed out in different directions, very un-Alex. "I married you, Daphne, and I'm not interested in letting you go."

"You sound so possessive," she murmured.

"I don't mean to come on too strong." He walked over and put the velvet pouch in her hand, clasping her fingers around it. "Please think about it."

"I don't know, Alex. I'm really exhausted, and it would be too easy to give in. I know in my heart that's the wrong thing to do." She was ready to give in now—if only she hadn't overheard their conversation. If only the doctor hadn't advised against more children. How could she stay with him knowing that she'd cheated him of the thing he'd married her for?

"Let's not talk anymore. You lie down," he said, helping her toward the bed. "I'm going to prove to you that I'm husband material you shouldn't throw out.''

She sighed, allowing him to lead her to the bed. For a second, when his hands touched her shoulders through the thin material of her nightgown, she wished things could be different. "Two weeks, Alex. That's all. On our anniversary, we sign divorce papers."

Was two weeks long enough to find out if they should stay married? Could she ever be convinced that she belonged with Alex, especially knowing her father had sold her along with his livestock?

A sudden wail pierced her thoughts.

"Where do you want this crib, ma'am?"

Alex's jaw dropped. Daphne, suddenly very businesslike, pointed to a section of the room near her bed. "Line all three up in a row right there at the foot of the bed, please."

"Wait a minute!" he thundered.

The staff paused instantly.

"What is going on here?" he demanded of Daphne.

"I'm setting up the nursery." She lifted her chin to meet his gaze without any sign of retreat in her eyes.

"The nursery is on the third floor of the house, where it's always been," he said carefully. Maybe she thought she was confined to this small wing of rooms, and that the babies had to stay with her.

"I know where it is, Alex. But my children need to be with me. Carry on, please," she said to Nelly and a few puffing young boys.

Alex stared as an insurmountable wall of baby cribs went up between him and Daphne. "Daphne, the babies have always stayed in the nursery."

"How do you know?" She cocked her head at him. "You were the only baby from your parents' marriage."

"I've seen pictures! I've heard Nelly talk about it. I was raised in the nursery!" Yes, their lives were different, but even Daphne should be able to comprehend that being married to him meant luxuries she should enjoy.

"My children aren't going to sleep in an attic, Alex," she said briskly. "They stay with me."

"But you're exhausted! You'd sleep better with them upstairs."

She gave him a wicked smile. "You said you'd help me. I'm assuming that also means with the babies. We'll be just fine."

With a regal nod, she dismissed Nelly and the other help. Three crying babies wiggled on the king-size bed, all wanting something. He had no idea what.

"Here now," she cooed. Swiftly, she let down her nightgown top and lifted a baby to her breast.

Cold prickles ran over the back of Alex's neck as he watched the baby latch on to the rose-colored nipple. His mouth dried out. *Whoa. Out of my element with that one.* Shifting from boot to boot, he wondered what he should do with the other two squalling babies.

"You can hold them and rock them in that chair," Daphne instructed. "They'll calm down long enough for me to feed this one."

With trepidation, he went to pick up one baby, very delicately. She fit into his arm like a well-wrapped package, instantly quieting at being picked up. With some difficulty, he hoisted the other one and fit her into the other arm as he sat. With his boot, he set the rocker to moving, but the babies seemed more interested in sticking their fists in their mouths. "I kind of like this," he said, pride growing in him.

"Good. If you're going to help me for two weeks, you'd better."

"Now, wait a minute. I said I wanted the chance to convince you that our marriage was worth saving. I didn't say I wanted to be a—"

"Father?" Daphne supplied. "Maybe you don't."

"I do," he cried, stung. "It's just that maybe you're deliberately going about this the hard way!"

She bristled before his eyes. "Meaning?"

"Meaning that the babies could be upstairs with the proper help they need, and we could get on with working our marriage out!" He glowered at her.

"I'm sorry, Alex. But I'm not going to have these babies and then toss them aside for someone else to raise. I know your definition of saving our marriage probably meant getting back into my bed, but as you can see, it is occupied. And will stay that way until the babies are older."

"How much older?" he demanded, frowning.

"I don't know how long I'll be able to nurse," she said honestly. "Though it's going very smoothly for me now, I've been told that the more tired I get, the more difficult it is, particularly with three. The milk supply may not be enough for what the babies need.

They're so new right now, they don't need much, mainly just the comfort of suckling. I'll have to see.''

He obviously wasn't going to be allowed that same comfort, Alex realized, with Daphne's bed full of his offspring. Despite the generous size of the bed, that left very little room for his six-two frame. Making love wasn't what he had in mind. But he did want to hold his wife, lie with her, be able to reach out in the night to assure himself she was where she belonged.

He had a sneaking suspicion Daphne didn't want him there, though. Briefly, he wondered if she'd insist on nursing just long enough to get past the two weeks they'd agreed upon.

A knock sounded peremptorily at the door. ''Your mother has arrived, Miss Daphne,'' Sinclair said. ''Where shall I put her suitcases?''

Great. Alex braced himself and his load by putting a boot against the bed rail and settled down as comfortably as possible with the babies waiting for their turn to nurse. Three babies, a wife who didn't want to be married to him and a mother-in-law in residence.

Bad odds for a man who'd drawn a supposedly lucky three of a kind.

Chapter Three

"Hello, Mrs. Way," Alex said congenially.

Daphne could tell by the look on his face that he wasn't pleased her mother had come to stay. But she needed her help, needed someone on her side.

"Hello, Alex," Danita Way replied warily.

"Put Mother's things in the room down the hall, please, Sinclair," she instructed.

He nodded and left the room. Daphne continued to nurse, trying to stay relaxed so her milk would flow. Her mother reached to take one of the babies from Alex and sat down, cooing to it.

"I think I'm ready to switch," Daphne told Alex. She handed him a nicely soothed baby, noting how swift he was to hand off the agitated, hungry child.

"Is there enough left for the other two?" Alex asked.

Daphne smiled tightly. "For now, yes. In the next couple of days, we'll know."

"Daphne's gotta be relaxed," Danita Way stated, with a meaningful look at him. "She needs six full weeks to recover just from having the babies, and then probably a whole year to get back up to strength. She doesn't need to be upset.''

"Mother," Daphne protested mildly.

"I don't want to upset her, Mrs. Way," Alex began.

"Danita," she informed him. "I'm here to help. We can all work together if need be. But last I heard you and Daphne was getting a divorce. Don't think much of 'em myself, but if that's what you want to do, it ain't none of my business. However, these babies are, and I won't have you upsetting my daughter. Or my grandbabies.''

"Mrs. Way!" Alex's boot slid from the bed rail to the floor. The baby in his arms, who had been so nicely soothed, flailed her fists momentarily and peered at him.

"Danita," she reminded him.

"Danita, the last thing I want is to upset your daughter. In fact, I don't even want to divorce her. I want to stay married. The divorce is her idea. At this point, I'm going along with whatever Daphne thinks is best, but I'm definitely not trying to upset her, even though I intensely dislike the idea of not being married to her.''

"He telling the truth?" Danita speared her daughter with a stare.

Daphne stirred uncomfortably, holding a baby against her as if she were a shield. "It isn't the way he makes it sound."

"So how is it?"

Daphne shrugged helplessly, refusing to meet Alex's gaze. "We can't stay married."

"Why can't we?" Alex demanded.

"Because of the babies." She could hardly bear to look at him, sitting in the rocker holding her child so gently. Why did he have to be so difficult? She couldn't stand knowing that she couldn't give him what he wanted. A woman wanted to be everything to her man. She couldn't be his dream come true.

"I was happy when I discovered we were having a child, Daphne. A bit sooner than we'd planned, and the fact that there were three did surprise me, but who can plan these things? I just always wanted you here with me."

"So what's the problem, Daphne?" Her mother eyed her suspiciously. "The man sounds serious to me."

"You don't understand," Daphne protested weakly. "He…Alexander Senior bought Daddy's livestock at a highly inflated price to help him out financially. It was a dowry. An expensive, twentieth-century dowry. Alexander Senior thought he was getting a good deal, Mother. Genes, basically. I can't bear staying married knowing it."

"Whoa, Daphne," Alex protested. "You've got this all wrong."

She shook her head at him. "No, I don't. I heard you talking to your father the day I came to tell you I was pregnant. You said then you weren't sure if the marriage would last."

"Did you say that?" Danita demanded.

"I don't know," Alex said slowly. "That's been many months ago. Daphne, I think I only meant that we needed time to be together, time to get to know each other without having the passel of kids Dad wanted underfoot.''

"Well, it didn't quite work out that way.'' Daphne raised her eyebrows at him in an exasperated manner.

"No, it didn't. But that doesn't mean we can't work it out. Not all marriages start on a perfect foundation. We at least have good materials to start with.''

She stared at him, wishing he weren't everything she'd always wanted in a man. Completely aware that her mother watched her with eagle eyes, Daphne decided she couldn't say what was bothering her the most. Sometime when she and Alex were alone, she would tell him exactly what had been the crowning blow in her decision to leave. But not right now. It hurt too much to say in front of another human being. Especially her mother, whose feelings would be hurt if she knew that Cos Way had been so underhanded as to sell his worst livestock to Alexander Senior. Daphne hadn't even been worth his good livestock. Cos had laughed himself silly over the "runt cows" he'd sold Alexander Banning. Overhearing her father's celebration, Daphne had burned with shame. Her father was underhanded, dishonest, a snake-oil salesman.

Alex had been forced to marry her on this foundation. Shaky it was, indeed. He'd only done it for his father, who had been so ill at the time.

Too bad they couldn't have foreseen Alexander Senior's rapid recovery. It could have saved them all a lot of heartache.

"Sounds like a tempest in a teapot to me, Daphne,'' her mother pronounced. "Alex has got his head on straight. He's a fine man. You just make up yer mind to stay married and quit all this gibbering about him not understanding the problem.'' As an aside, she said to Alex, ''She may have baby blues. It'll go off in time, but it's darn wearing while you got 'em. Makes ya hysterical and overly weepy.''

''Mother!'' Daphne exclaimed. Her hope of support was vanishing right before her eyes as she watched her mother siding with the enemy. ''I don't have baby blues. I'm not hysterical nor weepy!'' She burst into tears.

''Oh, no, Daphne, don't do that,'' Alex said, getting to his feet instantly and shifting the sleeping baby in his arms to one of the cribs. ''Honey, don't cry.''

She jerked away from the comforting arm he tried to put around her. ''Don't patronize me.'' Sniffling, she wiped her nose on her gown sleeve.

Alex quickly called for Nelly, who must have been hovering outside because she quickly popped into the room. ''Yes, Mr. Alex?''

''Can we have some handkerchiefs in here? I'm not sure this wing has been completely outfitted for—''

''Handkerchiefs!'' Daphne shot to her feet. ''Is there anything wrong with toilet paper? Do I have to wipe my nose on linen just because I'm living under your roof? Do people have to hover just to wipe my nose? Alex, my mother is here to take care of me, and she's all I want!'' She eyed him defiantly, and he backed up a step. Nelly dutifully shuffled out of the room. Daphne hoped she hadn't hurt Nelly's feelings, but she'd sort that out later. For now, she wanted one less person in the room.

''Why don't you give her a chance to finish nursing, Alex?'' Danita inquired kindly. ''I'll send for you when she's more rested.''

Daphne turned her back so he would leave.

''Okay,'' Alex agreed, though she could tell he was reluctant. ''Let me know if you need anything.''

A moment later, the door closed behind him and Daphne put the baby she'd been nursing in a crib and threw herself on the bed to cry.

''There, there,'' her mother said, patting her back. ''It's going to be all right, Daphne. You're just trying to do too much.''

''I only want some peace and quiet!'' she wailed. ''I don't want to be upset, I want enough breast milk for my babies. Is that so much to ask?''

''No, it's not,'' her mother soothed. ''Get some rest.''

''I have to feed the last baby!'' Daphne broke into fresh weeping, completely overwhelmed by her situation. It was Alex, it was the babies, it was her mother not understanding. But mostly it was Alex and the fact that her heart was breaking because she couldn't give him what he needed. It was worse than not having enough breast milk, though that was terribly difficult. She wanted to be an earth mother, giving her children good nutrition. She wanted to be a perfect wife, but that wasn't going to happen, either.

''She's gone to sleep already, Daphne. I honestly don't believe that one was as hungry, or maybe rocking put her to sleep. Rest now. In another two hours, you can try again.''

Daphne allowed herself to relax under her mother's

ministering hands. Unfortunately, as good as it felt to be comforted by her mother, she couldn't help wishing for her husband.

ALEX JUMPED as the door popped open. Danita stared at him. "I knew you'd be out here pacing. She's asleep."

"Good."

"Well, come on. Show me where the kitchen is," Danita told him. "I'm going to fix this baby a bottle, nursing or no. Daphne needs sleep, and sleep she's gonna get. This one's gonna get food, if she'll take it." She handed Alex a flailing body that smelled suspiciously like its diaper needed changing.

"Don't worry about the odor. I'll show you how to change a diaper in a minute." Danita bustled along behind him. "She's just about to let out a good shout, and I didn't want her waking Daphne up. That girl's determined to be everything to everybody, but she's stretched herself too thin this time."

Alex commanded himself to ignore the smell, though if the truth were to be known, he was rather fascinated by the thought that his child had made its first bowel movement in his presence. "I have a lot to learn about this baby business."

"I know. Don't we all." She moved into the kitchen and began banging through cabinets. "I had eight and I'm still gettin' educated. New gadgets, new thinking about a simple subject. Nowadays, folks have a baby and they gotta buy a library full of books to tell 'em how to talk to their kids and everything. Not as simple as it used ta be."

"Can I help you with something?" Nelly asked, somewhat timidly approaching Danita Way.

"Formula. Show me where the formula is."

Nelly shook her head worriedly. "We don't have any."

"Don't be silly. The hospital always sends some home."

"According to Sinclair, Daphne left hers at the hospital. Said she wasn't going to use it, and her share could be given to those less fortunate who needed extra."

Danita sighed in exasperation. "That's my daughter. Flying with her face in the wind and never looking back. Okay." She gave Alex a considering stare. "You've probably got a Mercedes or some such you drive around in, don'tcha?"

"Yes, I have a car," Alex replied, bewildered. If Daphne was "flying with her face in the wind," then her mother was the proverbial whirlwind of motion.

"Well, grab a car seat and let's get to the store." Danita hurried in the direction of the garage. "I'll show you the secret of soothing a fussy baby. You put the car seat in, and I'll fix this one's stinkiness." She took the baby from Alex and held it to her ample body. "And you sure know how to announce your presence, little lady. Reminds me of…never mind."

"Here's a diaper, Mrs. Way," Nelly said.

"Danita," she replied.

"And some wipes. I wouldn't mind doing that, if you'd let me," Nelly offered.

"And I wouldn't mind lettin' ya." Danita surrendered the infant to a grateful Nelly, whom Alex knew had been itching to get her hands on the babies. Daphne had been like a ferocious mother bear, not allowing anyone near her cubs. "I've been fully responsible for eight babies' clean backsides, and danged if I don't mind letting someone else help me."

"Car seat's in." It had been a bit of a battle, and he'd nearly called Sinclair to explain how the contraption worked, but he had finally gotten it positioned properly.

Danita took the freshened baby from Nelly and popped it into the car seat, then got in next to it. Alex started the engine as Nelly leaned in the window.

"It's up to you, Ms. Way, but Daphne insists only cloth diapers touch her babies' skin. She says it's healthier, and environmentally conscious."

"She's right, my Daphne is," Danita said. "I'll pick up a case of plastic diapers while I'm in the store. Hurry, Alex. Get the car started so the baby'll settle. I swear, Daphne's got ears like a bat. She'll hear this baby crying and there'll be no keeping her down."

Alex backed the sports car down the driveway. As he hit the main road in front of the ranch and gathered speed, the baby miraculously quit crying. "Whew. That's something, isn't it?"

"Not really. This 'un's got a stomachache. She's not hungry, just gassy. She wouldn't have nursed even if Daphne had tried to. She might as well be sleeping."

"I see." Alex watched her in the mirror. "Do you think we're smart to circumvent what Daphne wants for the babies? You did say we shouldn't upset her."

Danita shrugged. "Daphne's a great girl, a real go-getter. Determined as hell—heck," she said in deference to the sleeping baby. "But she don't know squat about babies. The first month these critters are gonna poop stuff that doesn't even resemble poop, and they do it constantly. It's really better if we handle this a little differently, at least for the first month." She sighed as Alex pulled into the grocery store lot. "Parents are always overwrought with their first kiddos."

"She's got a lot to deal with." Alex searched for a parking spot.

"Be better if she could do things the easy way, but not my Daph. All my children are stubborn. Like me."

"Probably a good trait."

"Yep. Your father's stubborn, too."

"Like a mule." Alex could agree with that.

"'Course, only one of ya's gonna be able to be stubborn all the way," she said, "it's either gonna be you or Daphne. Else the marriage doesn't work out."

He shut off the car and turned to face her. "Do you have any suggestions?"

"Let her be the stubborn one," Danita suggested. "Gonna be tough for you, 'cause you got the old man's personality, and he's an ornery son of a gun. But let Daphne be the stubborn one, and you just might keep her."

"She's determined to leave me."

"Nah. What'd I tell ya, Alex? She's gotta do everything the hard way. Whether it's breast-feeding, which most woman tire out feeding one, Daphne's

gotta do three. And diapers. She's gotta be environmentally conscious. It's the same in her marriage.
She's got a bug in her bonnet that she's not perfect
enough for ya. Dig in your heels and prove to her that
you two are right for each other, all the while telling
her she's right.''

"It sounds so underhanded," he murmured.

"Yep. Runs in our family a bit. I call it learning
to get along with folks.'' Danita gave him a huge
smile. "Now. You run in there and get some soybean
formula. This one's farting up a storm, and that tells
me maybe her and cow's milk ain't gonna be a good
thing. Get Daphne some roses while you're at it. She
likes big yellow ones that look like the sun. I can't
stand that damn dreary room, all those cribs crowded
in there like buses. Your family's rich as Croesus, she
can have the help I could never afford, and by heaven,
I'm gonna make her take advantage of it.''

He grinned at her. "Why do I get the feeling you're
on my side?''

"I'm on both your sides." She pecked him with a
gnarly finger. "It behooves me greatly not to have
any of my children divorcing. It's bad economy when
there's three newborns involved. Pick me up a box of
chocolate Turtles while you're in there," she instructed. "I can tell I'm gonna be needed for a
while.''

DAPHNE AWAKENED to the sound of silence. She
yawned, realizing she was sweating. Her gown was
twisted between her legs, constricting her. Her breasts

hurt, but she felt relaxed for the first time since the babies had been born.

The babies! They needed to eat! She shot up in the bed and flew to the cribs. Every single one was empty.

Throwing on a robe, she hurried down the hall. Stopping just in time before exposing herself to the whole contingent of people standing in the great room, she watched the lesson in progress.

Nelly and Danita were patiently showing Alex how to diaper a baby. By the pile of plastic diapers beside him, he wasn't any good at it. Sinclair stood nearby, holding one child who waited its turn at being a victim to Alex's technique. Alexander Senior scowled in a corner, apparently disapproving of his son's participation in child rearing.

"I got it!" Alex cried triumphantly. Holding the baby up, he showed off his handiwork to an admiring group. The diaper promptly slid off, leaving the baby bare, which was cute, except then a trickle splattered to the table underneath. Nelly quickly clapped a washcloth to the infant bottom.

"Maybe a little more work," she said kindly. "This one has a tiny waist. It's hard to get it to fit properly."

Daphne slapped her hand over her mouth so she wouldn't laugh at Alex's forlorn expression. Part of her was angry that they were putting plastic diapers on her babies, but if Alex was bent and determined to learn how to diaper, then plastic tabs were certainly safer than safety pins.

The yearning inside her, the voice she was desperately trying to ignore, told her that he was the most wonderful man in the world for wanting to learn. The pile of diapers and torn tabs beside him was testament to his determination. These girls his father regarded as nice but not as important as boys appeared to have Alex's complete interest—despite the fact that she couldn't give him a son.

If she wasn't careful, she wouldn't be able to insist upon the divorce in two weeks. She'd tried putting three cribs in the room to distance Alex. It wasn't working, she knew, her heart melting as he finally succeeded with a well-wrapped diaper and snuggled his daughter to him in masculine victory. She'd brought in her mother as a deterrent, but that didn't seem to be working, either, as she watched Danita thump her son-in-law on the back in congratulations.

Their marriage was based on lies. Her father had lied, cheating Alexander Senior. Alexander Senior had lied, cheating Alex out of a wife of his choosing. Alex was lying, really, by saying it didn't matter that he didn't have a son, that he'd married her because he loved her. He'd married her because his father wanted him to. Alexander Senior would really roar if he knew the overpriced cattle he'd bought by way of a dowry hadn't secured him what he'd thought he was really buying—male heirs.

Even she wasn't being truthful, insisting she wanted a divorce. It was the last thing in the world she wanted, and what she was most determined to get. One day Alex would look back regretfully upon his life with her. He would want more than she had given him. She'd be kidding herself to think it could work out differently.

"Alex," she said as she walked into the great room, "may I see you alone for a moment?"

The whole room came to a standstill to stare at her.

"The nap looks like it did you good," Danita said.

"I'm fine, Mother. Alex? Do you have a moment?" She refused to be turned from her purpose.

"Sure." He followed her down the hall to the bedroom full of cribs.

"You have diapered my babies in disposable diapers. You have taken them from my room. I said I would raise my children without an army of staff, and I meant it. This isn't Windsor Castle, and I am not a princess who wants to be waited on hand and foot."

"You needed your rest, Daphne. It's important for, uh, breast-feeding," he said quickly.

He'd been coached, she could tell. Her mother's work, no doubt. "Alex, I absolutely will not become dependent on you. If you can't go along with what I think is best for me and my family, then we'll just have to move out."

She watched anger flare brightly into his midnight blue eyes.

"Daphne, you've avoided me for months. You've kept me dangling on a string about a divorce. You've had the audacity to think you can keep my children from me. As the other half of this marriage, I have some rights, too. It's been pointed out to me that I should let your female hormones rule for the time being, but—" he caught her in a grip Daphne had no desire to shrug off "—right now, I've had all the advice I can take."

With that, he slanted his mouth against hers, kissing her in a way that sent memories washing over her and desire flaming into her body.

Breathlessly, she sagged against him as he raised his head to stare at her. "No protest?"

"I'm working on one," she said feebly. "Maybe I'll go take a shower."

"Good idea. I'll help you." Lifting her in his arms as if she were no more than a feather, Alex carried her into the bathroom.

"No! I'm not showering with you!" she cried.

"I didn't suggest that you should." He pulled her gown over her head, staring at her body so intensely that Daphne could only pray he wouldn't find fault with her. "Though, as I recall, you liked it very much when I washed your back. And front. You're so beautiful," he told her, kissing each breast reverently. "Those little ladies of mine are going to have to learn to share."

"Oh, Alex," Daphne murmured, as he licked her nipples into taut, swollen eagerness. "Don't do this to me."

Slowly, he raised his head and moved away from her. "You're right. I'm rushing you. I've thought about you day and night, Daphne. Damn it, I've missed you!"

"I've missed you, too," she said quietly. Their marriage had been so good until she'd overheard his conversation with his father.

"So. No more talk about divorce." He gave her a

look that meant he intended to have the last word on this.

"On the contrary," she said miserably, "I find it more necessary than ever to get a divorce. It's even more imperative that I move out of the house. You've just proven to me that we can't live together under the same roof without wanting each other. There's no in-between for us, Alex. It's better if I move back to my apartment as soon as possible."

Chapter Four

Slowly, Alex reached for Daphne's robe and helped wrap it around her. He kept his expression neutral, but his heart pounded. "Tell me what you're so afraid of."

She shook her head. "I'm not afraid." But she backed up a step from him, belying her words.

"You are. You're practically shivering now." Even though he knew she wouldn't like it, he reached across the space between them and took her hands in his, rubbing them gently between his palms. "All this insistence on a divorce isn't good for us, Daphne."

"I know," she said, her tone miserable, "but I think it would be better than living like this." After a second, she pulled her hands out of his and turned around.

He stared at the white, quilted material of her bathrobe, wondering how he could get her to understand the way he felt. "I apologize for coming on too strong. I have always been greatly...attracted to you."

"It's okay," she whispered.

"But don't do it again?"

Her hair shook in a tantalizing fall of amber brightness. "No, don't do it again."

He drew a deep breath. "Daphne, you are an amazingly beautiful woman. You are my wife. I'd have to be six feet under not to want you. But if that's what you want, I swear on my honor not to touch you."

They'd made so many promises to each other when they'd married. Daphne bit her lip, refusing to let the tears fall. "And you won't fight me when I move out in fourteen days?"

"I won't, if that's your decision." He'd help her, though the effort would kill him. Under no circumstances would his wife suffer if he could help it. "I'll expect joint custody, however."

She whirled, her face pale. "What does that mean?"

His shrug was dismissive, a gesture he forced. "You're trying to separate me completely from your life, Daphne. You may be willing to live without me, but it's a decision I don't think our children will feel the same about."

An exhausted breath left her. "I can't fight with you any more right now, Alex. I'm too tired."

Her green eyes didn't sparkle with their usual fire. Beating her down wasn't going to help either of them or the babies. And intimidating her wasn't something he wanted to do, either. Desperation had made him speak the truth, though he'd known she wasn't ready to hear it. He nodded and walked to the door. "Get some rest. Ring if you need anything."

She stared at him with huge, almond-shaped eyes. He inclined his head to her before leaving the room.

Brilliant move, Alex. Danita's advice was good, but he hadn't followed it very well. It was difficult where Daphne was concerned! She made him feel so many things all at once that it was impossible to remember he was supposed to be allowing her to be the stubborn one. He wanted to hold her. He wanted to kiss her all over that wonderful body, hear the sighs he'd missed hearing. But when she pushed him away he felt rejected. It sent some macho monster rearing inside him, which was exactly what he didn't need right now. Daphne never responded well to hard-pressure tactics. It was a lesson he should have learned well. After all, she had moved and gotten an unlisted number to avoid him.

Completely frustrated, he sought out Sinclair. He soon located him, polishing the car Alex had driven to the store to get diapers and formula with Danita. It hardly needed sprucing up, but his faithful butler's movements were a bit frantic.

"This is not going well, Sinclair," he said, leaning against the car near an open can of wax.

"No, sir."

Alex sighed. He reached for a chamois cloth and dipped it into the wax.

"Allow me, sir," Sinclair told him. He took the chamois and put it aside.

"Trust me, I could use the work, Sinclair."

"You don't do it as well as I do."

His butler's craggy face was impassive. Alex folded his arms across his chest and looked at the sky. Daphne was telling him the same thing. Only she could raise their children the way she wanted it done.

"I don't know," he murmured. "I have to fit in somehow."

"You've got your hands full."

The understatement of the year. Alex nodded. "How's my father enjoying watching me struggle?"

"Mr. Banning seems quite astounded by the pandemonium which has broken out in the house. But I think he's getting used to it. He was actually talking about buying Miss Daphne a gift."

"Hope he does better than I did with the pearls."

"Miss Daphne did not receive them well?" Sinclair raised his brows.

"She hardly received them at all. I think they're still lying on the dresser in their pouch," Alex said, his tone rueful.

"I see." Sinclair rubbed harder at an invisible spot on the car. "Perhaps there's something Miss Daphne would like better."

"I don't know what," Alex replied heavily, "unless it's a divorce. She mentions that quite frequently."

"I'm positive it will come to you, sir."

"What will?" His state of confusion was growing. How could he think when Daphne had scrambled his normally acute mind?

"The right thing to do."

"You're not much help except for mumbling platitudes," Alex told him grumpily.

"No, sir."

Alex shifted, knowing he was being a pain. The problem was, he felt like his skin wasn't his own. He felt like he didn't fit into his own house any longer.

"Should I go see my father? Would he welcome a visit?"

"Not right now." Sinclair's voice was kind yet matter-of-fact. "He's revising his will with his attorney."

"Revising his will!" Alex straightened. "Why?"

Sinclair shrugged. "I am not party to the innermost thoughts of my employer, sir."

"The hell you're not! You know all my innermost thoughts, and I'm your employer, too!"

"I helped diaper you. That gives me special rights in your life, I suppose," Sinclair said good-naturedly. "However, your father and I have always had a different sort of relationship."

"You're not the only one." Alex squinted at the top level of rooms. He thought he could see his father's shadow move from the dormered window. "He didn't tell you anything?"

"Not a thing," Sinclair confirmed. "But I would think any changes he has decided to make have to do with your three new daughters."

"Daughters. Of course. Father's probably cutting me out of his will."

"Could be." Sinclair's tone wasn't encouraging. "Though I felt hopeful when he touched Alex Junior's head."

"He did?" He couldn't help his astonishment.

"When he thought Nelly and I weren't looking, he actually rubbed one palm over Alex Junior's head." Sinclair wore a questioning frown. "Since she lacks even fuzz up there, I was quite shocked."

"She is the ugliest baby on earth, isn't she?"

Alex's shoulders drooped. "A runt. That's what she reminds me of. How could I father a runt?"

Sinclair started laughing. He dropped his chamois onto the gleaming car and turned to lean against it, holding his stomach with laughter.

"What? What's so funny?" Alex demanded.

His usually reserved butler shook his head, wiping tears from his eyes. Alex stared, astonished. "I've never seen you act this way."

Sinclair bent over double, guffawing in a most unaustere manner.

"Will you please tell me what you're laughing about?"

Sinclair took out a handkerchief and wiped his eyes. "That's just what your father said when you were born."

Alex froze. "I see nothing funny about that." His father had taunted him most of his life about numerous things. He couldn't remember ever really pleasing him. To be reminded of his shortcomings right now, when he'd fathered three girls, wasn't something he wanted to hear.

"No, probably not." Sinclair gave him an ironic look and pulled his wallet from his suit pocket. He unfolded it, then handed it to him. "That's really what I'm laughing about."

He stared at the picture underneath the worn plastic. A baby face peered out at him. "You have an ugly baby, too?" It was something he didn't know about Sinclair. He thought the man's whole life had revolved around Alex since the day he'd been born. But maybe there was a happy ending to the story.

Maybe Sinclair's ugly offspring had grown up to be someone wonderful, a man with intelligence and great abilities—

"That's you," Sinclair said with a grin. "Look closer. That little runt is you." He reached to pull the picture from under the plastic so Alex could see better. "Bald as a baseball bat, despite Nelly rubbing your head with baby oil constantly. Just like rubbing a baking potato with butter," he said cheerfully.

The baby in the picture seemed happy in his ugliness, sporting a satisfied expression as he lay snuggled into his covers. Alex felt a momentary sting for the baby's unspoiled happiness. He'd had no idea what he was up against.

"No hair, didn't open your eyes for days," Sinclair went on. "Just a happy runt, content to be fed every couple of hours, then you went right back to sleep. Nelly said she'd never seen such a good baby." He folded the picture away. "Your mother thought you were the most beautiful thing she'd ever laid eyes on," he said with a meaningful glance at Alex.

"She did?"

"She did, right until the day she died." Sinclair gave him a swift pat on the back. "Your mother didn't care two hoots what the old man thought about her baby. She said runts were blessings, too, and if you were a bit small and a lot ugly, that just made you all the more special in her eyes."

"I'm sure Father had plenty to say about that," Alex muttered.

"Nothing your mother ever listened to. When he complained because you had a lazy eye that needed surgery, she told him to take a flying leap. She phrased it more ladylike, but that was the gist. And when you needed special shoes because your feet turned different ways, your mother told your father it meant you would always walk a more gifted path.'' Sinclair began putting away the can of wax and the rags. ''Guess she was right.''

''She sounds like Daphne,'' Alex said with sudden realization.

''She does, doesn't she?''

He sounded surprised, but Alex had the idea that Sinclair had been leading up to his point.

''And your father loved your mother to distraction.''

''He did?'' Alex couldn't imagine his father loving anyone enough to be distracted.

''Yes. 'Course, he couldn't show it much. Your father hadn't experienced enough love in his life to be able to show it to anyone else.'' Sinclair finished packing the tools. ''It's a sin of the father I might recommend you not visit on your own marriage,'' he said cryptically.

Alex stared at him.

''And as you may have realized from seeing the very picture made the day you were born in the hospital, runts grow up with feelings and needs of their own. Alex Junior will need you to treat her as if she were the most beautiful child in the world, just as your mother did you. Though I daresay Miss Daphne is going to have to come up with better names for those children soon before I lose my wits,'' he muttered before nodding briskly and leaving, the only lecture he'd ever given Alex apparently over.

It was a lot to think about. Alex squinted at the dormered window again, his father's shadow more evident than before. That was how he always saw his father, as an overwhelming, disapproving, dark presence that affected his life. He loved his father, knew how to deal with him on most matters. But the old man was an enigma. He had never really expended sentiment on Alex, not with the fond affection Sinclair and Nelly had shown him. They had raised him, of course.

It struck him that he had suggested to Daphne that she do the same by telling her the babies should go to the nursery. That had been an error on his part, one he resolved not to repeat. If his mother hadn't died when he was so young, he doubted very seriously that Sinclair and Nelly would have had such a great hand in his upbringing, as wonderful as they'd been to him.

But family retainers, close and part of the family as they were, couldn't replace a father's and mother's love to their children. He stared at the shining, polished surface of his sports car and made a sudden decision.

DAPHNE SHOWERED and took a nap, so she was ready when her mother brought the young troop of hungry mouths in to be fed. Eagerly, she reached for Yoda, who was crying the most urgently.

"Oh, sweet thing," she murmured, taking the baby in her arms. "Are you hungry?"

"They're all hungry," Danita said. She sat in a

rocker with the other two and held them to her ample bosom. "Flowers look nice," she said over the wails.

"Yes." Daphne barely glanced at the vase of sunshine-yellow roses Alex had brought into her room. It was too painful. To continue her stern facade, she couldn't allow herself to be softened by his attempts to woo her. She wished he would stop so she could continue feeling hurt and angry, the way she'd been when she'd left this house before. Lying back against the pillow, she forced herself to think of anything besides Alex so she could relax enough to feed her baby.

Ten minutes later, Danita gave Miss Magoo to her. "Will you ever grow eyelashes?" she cooed to Miss Magoo as the baby latched on.

Danita glanced up from changing Yoda into a fresh gown and diaper. "Sure, she will. You didn't have any lashes when you were born."

"I didn't?" She hardly needed to use mascara now.

"Nope, you didn't. In fact, I think that 'un looks most like you."

"Do you think so?" She gazed at the contentedly feeding baby. "Her hair does seem to have a little red in it."

"Yep. Gonna have your green eyes, too."

"How can you tell?" Right now, all the babies' eyes seemed about the same color to her, not that she'd really gotten a good look at them.

Danita shrugged, picked Yoda up then set her down cozily in her crib. She returned to grab Alex Junior up and seat herself in the rocker. "I don't know. She just looks like you when you were born."

"Well, I'm glad for that." She held her baby tightly.

"This 'un looks like Alex." Danita looked at the baby she held.

"I don't know," she replied doubtfully, "I don't see much of Alex's, um, good looks in her." She wasn't about to mention to her mother that she found her husband very handsome!

"You'll see."

Since Danita seemed certain of that, Daphne nodded. "What about that one? Do you see anybody in her?"

They both stared at the crib where Yoda was sleeping.

"Yes. To be honest, I see a lot of Sabrina Caroline in her."

Tears jumped into Daphne's eyes. Sabrina had been Alex's mother. Daphne could only remember meeting her once, at a Christmas party. It had been the only year her family had been invited to the lavish party at the Green Forks ranch, because Mrs. Banning died the next year. And the feud had begun. Her father and Alex's father had spent years arguing over fence lines and water rights and steers crossing where they shouldn't... Daphne made herself stop thinking about it. She felt uncomfortable enough in this house as it was. "I suppose it will please Alex," she said wistfully, "to have a child who looks like his mother."

"Not until he realizes it." Danita gave her daughter a jaundiced look.

Daphne shook her head. "I'm not going to mention his mother. I don't even want to talk to Alex."

"You're not going about this the right way, Daphne Way," her mother warned. "You oughta think about how you'd really feel if Alex decided to give you what you say you want." Danita rocked in the chair. "Don't think you'd like it as much as you think you would."

"I don't think I would like it!" Daphne cried, distressed. "I think it's the only way. How can I stay married to a man who promised his father he would give him a son?"

"Bah. Alexander doesn't know girls from boys except for that which dangles tweenst their legs."

"Mother!"

"Well, it's true. Reckon if you'd dressed Alex Junior up in a blue onesie and booties and told Alexander it was a boy, he'da not known the difference. Sure as heck never held his own child, I'd be willing to bet." She stared at the baby in her arms. "Wish I'd thought of dressing you in blue sooner, tyke."

"Mother!" Daphne repeated, her tone more shocked than before. "I would never dress my daughters up to fool Mr. Banning. Children should be treated equally, no matter their sex."

"Well, you like to do things the hard way, Daphne, not that I'm suggesting we shoulda done it. I'm just saying I wish I'd thought of it sooner." Her expression was serious. "Maybe it would have kept the chauvinistic old idiot from calling his lawyer in."

Daphne's skin turned chilly. The baby allowed Daphne's nipple to slide out of her mouth in a satisfied, sleepy movement, but Daphne's insides were nowhere as content. "Lawyer?"

"Yep." Danita reached for Miss Magoo and traded her for a quiet, wide-eyed Alex Junior. "Nelly told me he's got the lawyer in there right now, and she heard him tell Sinclair he's changing his will."

"Oh, my," Daphne breathed. "Wonder what he's up to?"

"I have no idea." Danita competently diapered the baby and moved her to a crib. She gazed at the two sleeping babies, making certain their blankets covered them just so. "Don't think he's too happy with Alex, though. Shot blanks as far as the old tyrant is concerned."

"Mother, Mr. Banning is your age," she protested mildly. But her mind was going at a nervous clip. Surely Alex's father wouldn't punish him through his will just because his only son had given him nothing but granddaughters? "This baby never eats," she murmured, too unsettled to stay on one subject. "All she does is gaze around."

Danita came over to stare at the baby. "I know. She hardly cries, either. Won't surprise me if she sleeps through the night tonight, while the other two give us a run for our money."

"You think there's something wrong with her?" Daphne's heart jumped wildly with worry.

"Nope. Think she's got her daddy's mild-mannered constitution." Danita took the baby from Daphne and changed its diaper. "Maybe you need a clean bottom before you eat, tyke."

Daphne pulled her nightgown together as she considered her mother's words. Alex didn't have a mild-mannered constitution, as far as she was concerned. Or maybe it was *where* she was concerned.

Or maybe it was something she brought out in him.

Certainly, she had been drawn to Alex's rock-solid steadiness from the start. He was so stable, where she tended to float with the planetary alignment of the day. How could a son like Alex not please his father, even one as demanding as Alexander?

By not giving him what he'd requested on his deathbed, an annoying little voice reminded her. *She* was Alex's only failing. But he was like his mother, Sabrina, too kind to allow the poor farming family down the way to be left out of Christmas festivities. It hadn't been her nature.

It wasn't Alex's nature to throw the poor farming family out now just because he'd gotten sold a bill of goods he hadn't needed.

"What am I going to do?" she moaned, her mind feeling turned inside out.

"I don't know, Daphne Way. All I do know is you're in a bit of a pickle this moment." Her mother bustled about the room, then put the baby in Daphne's arms. Alex Junior gazed at her with wise, somber eyes.

"What do you think she wants?" Daphne asked her mother helplessly. "She's waiting for something, but I don't know what."

Danita scratched her head. "Tell you the truth, I don't think she knows what to do with those big bosoms of yours. I think that baby's kinda overwhelmed."

"That's one way she's not like her daddy, then." Daphne's face flamed.

"Didn't reckon so." Danita squinted at the baby. "You know, that 'un toots constantly. She's like a little bag of wind letting off a valve. Think it makes her too uncomfortable to eat."

"What am I going to do?"

"Maybe only a bottle is gonna do for that one, Daph." Danita sat on the bed. "I gave her some soy formula earlier, and she seemed to like it just fine. Those two babies, they appear to prefer the breast, but this one—"

"Mom!" Daphne exclaimed. "I am not feeding this child soy formula. She's going to need all the extra help she can get. Breast milk is better, especially when she's so tiny."

"Yes, but that baby doesn't want to feed. You want a hungry, colicky baby who for whatever reason can't tolerate your milk, or one that'll grow up just fine on soy?" Her mother shot her an impatient look. "Daphne Way, you're gonna have to learn to compromise one day, and by your daddy's long johns, at whose knee you learned this stubbornness, it ain't gonna be easy. But you're gonna have to learn to do it or you're gonna end up one unhappy lady."

"I just don't want to put a latex nipple in my baby's mouth," Daphne protested. "As small as she is, she needs all the natural protection my breast milk can give her."

"I agree. I'm just saying maybe it's not going to work with this one."

"I find it hard to believe the child that most resembles its father wouldn't be attracted to my breasts,'' Daphne grumbled. "Would you mind bringing me a bottle of the soy, then? I'm determined to prove you wrong.''

"Fine by me.''

Danita exited the room and returned about five minutes later to hand her a warm bottle. Daphne sighed in long-suffering patience, barely touching the nipple to Alex Junior's lips. The baby continued to stare at her. "See? This baby just doesn't want to eat anything.''

A nice, long burst of wind erupted from the region of the baby's diaper. Daphne met Danita's eyes in amazement. To her astonishment, the baby let out a demanding wail. Daphne lowered the bottle to Alex Junior's lips, and the baby began suckling with enthusiasm.

"She would have taken my breast if she hadn't already seen the bottle,'' Daphne said without much conviction.

"Maybe.'' Not even bothering to appear convinced, Danita walked to the window and stared down. Something below had obviously caught her attention.

"What is it?''

Her mother nodded at someone or something on the ground. "I'm not sure. Here,'' she said, reaching for Alex Junior, "let me take this 'un. Nelly's had a yen to feed one of these babies, and she and I can have a nice chat.''

Danita snatched the baby from her before Daphne had a chance to argue. "Brush your hair, Daphne,'' she commanded, ''and don't forget your teeth.'' Then she hurried from the room.

Daphne's mouth dropped open. ''For heaven's sake!'' What had gotten into her mother? She got out of bed and ran to the window, but saw nothing out of the ordinary. Just a lot of cars, which were always parked at the Banning mansion. She wondered if her mother had seen the Banning solicitor leaving. Maybe that's what she wanted, to hurry off to pick Nelly's brains about whatever Mr. Banning had been revising in his will.

She shook her head and went into the bathroom to comb her hair, tied it with a green ribbon, then took a moment to brush her teeth and wash her face. She felt so much better, she decided to step in front of the full-length mirror on the back of the door. It would be so nice if her stomach was beginning to shrink, though she'd never again have the body Alex had fallen in love with in the first place....

''Daphne?''

She gasped at the sound of his voice in the bedroom and slammed the bathroom door firmly closed. ''Yes?''

''Uh, do you have a second?''

''No!'' She'd left her nightgown and panties on the other side of the door when she decided to peek in the mirror.

There was silence for a moment.

''I'd like to talk to you.''

She closed her eyes at the soft huskiness of his voice. ''I'm listening.''

"I mean face-to-face. I don't want to wake the babies."

"Oh." She thought rapidly. "Well, come back in five minutes."

"Okay," he said, his tone uncertain. "Better yet, why don't you meet me on the front step in five? I really need to speak with you."

"Oh, okay." Maybe it had something to do with his father's will. If Alex suggested she move out with him, somewhere far away, like Alaska, she would do it in a flash. Anything not to have to live under his father's disapproving eye—

No. That wasn't right. She would never force Alex to choose between her and his birthright. "I'll be right there." Waiting to hear his footsteps as he walked away, Daphne told herself that the fact she'd agreed so readily to meet him wasn't a sign that her self-control was weakening. Dangerously.

"TROUBLE'S BREWING up there," Nelly intoned.

Nelly, Sinclair and Danita sat around a chopping block table in the middle of a large, well-organized kitchen. They took turns holding Alex Junior, their faces morose.

"Mr. Banning's changing his will, Alex is determined to win a woman who don't want him, and Daphne's not about to bend. We got girl babies out the wazoo that the old man finds unacceptable, all named after ugly creatures except Alex Junior, but she backfires like an old jalopy. What else can go wrong?" Danita inquired, not looking like she expected anyone to have an answer.

She cradled the baby closer. "I think Alex just brought home a gift." Her voice conveyed her worry.

"A gift!" Nelly and Sinclair stared at her.

"Yes, bless him, an expensive one. I'm pretty certain it's for Daphne, 'cause I saw him on the grounds outside and he motioned me to keep quiet." Danita sighed heavily and stared at the baby, who gazed at her as if she was listening to every word.

"Gifts are good," Sinclair said cautiously. "Wouldn't you both agree?"

"Gifts are good," Danita agreed, "but Daphne doesn't want gifts right now. She wants reassurance, and money can't buy that. Unfortunately, if my eyes weren't playing tricks on me, Alex brought home a doozy. I've got a funny feeling. Trouble's brewing."

Chapter Five

"What do you mean, this is for me?" Daphne put a trembling hand over her heart as she stared at the Rolls-Royce limousine and the respectful chauffeur standing beside it. Surely Alex was joking—

"You need your own driver and car." Alex grinned, obviously proud of his gleaming present. "This is big enough to fit all the babies into, and a few of their friends when they're ready for playmates."

"I...I—" Daphne closed her mouth, too astonished to speak. She looked from her happy soon-to-be ex-husband to the long, shiny limousine. "I don't know what to say."

The chauffeur wasn't going to say anything. He'd ducked his cap at her respectfully, then kept his eyes fixed forward as if he were a guard at Buckingham Palace. And Alex wasn't saying anything as he waited for her to express her happiness. But she wasn't! Was something wrong with her, that she couldn't appreciate the thoughtfulness behind his gesture?

"Alex," she whispered frantically, carefully watching to see if the chauffeur's gaze would flicker.

It didn't, so she continued. "Can I talk to you? Alone?"

"We are alone, Daphne."

By his standards, she supposed they were. Glancing guiltily toward the silent driver, she whispered, "Is he allowed a break? I mean, can he go get a cup of coffee or something?" She met Alex's eyes nervously. "I don't think I can communicate with a uniformed guard in my vicinity."

"Okay, Daphne."

Alex directed the driver toward the back entrance where he could find the kitchen. She kept her gaze focused on the grass at her feet, embarrassed.

"What is it?" Alex asked after the chauffeur was gone.

She didn't want to hurt his feelings, but she couldn't live with a driver who looked like Mussolini and a tank transporting her and her brood! "Alex, you can't be serious that this is for me."

His eyes were gentle as he looked at her. "Why not? Don't you like it?"

"Well...well, actually no." Miserably, she shook her head.

"Daphne, you're not supposed to be driving for a while," he said reasonably. "And you have to have a way to get the babies around."

"I...guess so." Sniffling, she realized she was trying not to cry. Why hadn't she considered the difference in their life-styles when she'd fallen in love with Alex?

It wouldn't have done a bit of good if she had. Drooping, she said, "I appreciate what you're trying to do for me. I'm so sorry, Alex, but...I can't accept your gift.''

"Why not?"

Daphne forced herself to look up. "It's just not me in the least.''

"How do you know, if you haven't given it a try?'' He pulled her into his arms. "Daph, listen. I want the best for you. I want you and the girls safe. This is the way all the children from the best families live. They go to the best private schools. They have the best doctors and clothes and everything.''

"I'm from one of the best families,'' Daphne interjected. "I really consider mine one of the best I've ever seen.''

"I know,'' he said hurriedly. "I shouldn't have put it that way. I meant, uh—''

"I know what you meant,'' Daphne interrupted impatiently. "I just want you to think for a minute. You and I have different ways, and it doesn't necessarily mean yours is always going to be better.''

"What can you possibly find to object to about having your own car?'' Alex's tone was brisk. "You and the children will have privacy and security this way.''

"And they won't see the world, and the world won't be able to see them!'' Daphne snapped. She tried to struggle out of Alex's hold, but he wouldn't allow it.

"Have you ever considered that the babies could be targets of kidnapping attempts because of the family they come from?''

Her skin prickled all over. She stared at him. "Of course not!"

He pulled her to the Rolls, opened the door, sat on the seat and pulled her into his lap. "Daphne, it's not uncommon for very wealthy children to—"

"Don't say it!" she cried. "Alex, this isn't what I want! I can't even think about my babies being in danger." The tears that clouded her eyes couldn't be helped.

"I can't, either," he told her, holding her tightly, yet gently. "Or you, for that matter." He took a tense breath. "I've thought a lot about how I could show you that I care about you, and yes, even entice you into staying married to me. But what I always come back to is that I've got four beautiful ladies I have to look out for, and while it may feel like I'm smothering you—or trying to buy you—I'm really trying to protect you." He hesitated for a second. "It's not unusual for a man to give the woman he marries a car, Daph. You can't go around in your mom's old VW forever."

It was a vintage sixties bug, completely in tune with her life-style—as it had been. She glanced around the smooth, expensive interior of the car. If she didn't know better, she'd think the smoky glass of the windows was bulletproof. "Alex, I can't live like this. I'd rather move back into my apartment. I want my children to grow up normally, in public schools and public parks, not in a fishbowl with Mafia-tinted windows."

They saw things so differently. It hadn't been this way, this divisive, when they'd fallen in love. All she'd known was that Alex Banning was a man who kept her happy, a man who made her feel alive and that all was in order.

Now she was all out of whack, all internally askew.

Lightly, her fingers traced the luxurious seat. There was any number of electronic functions she could push at her slightest whim. There was enough room inside to throw a party. Still, she felt like a genie in a bottle, and she needed to escape.

Alex stared at her, obviously disappointed and worried. Her mother had said she needed to compromise, and she hadn't wanted to do much of that in order to keep Alex at arm's length. But Danita was right. She really wanted him, and even if they weren't right for each other, she didn't want him wearing the unhappy expression he wore right now. She loved him too much, in spite of their differences.

"Alex?" she said softly.

"Yes?" His voice was hopeful, even eager.

"I'm going to suggest a compromise."

"You're not." He sounded sardonically surprised, which made her grin.

"If I let you give me a car—and that's my part of the compromise," she said with a wicked smile, "I'd like to suggest something I'm sure you'll find a little bit novel."

"Only a little bit?" He raised his brows.

"Well, maybe." She got out of his lap and pulled him toward the mansion. "Come on. I've got to change."

AN HOUR LATER, Alex found himself on a used-car lot, seated next to Daphne, who was at the steering wheel of a Chevy Suburban. The babies wailed or slept in their carriers, positioned on bench seats in the huge vehicle, which Alex couldn't see being practical at all. Nelly, Sinclair and Danita fit themselves around the baby carriers as best they could. A salesman stood outside the door, staring at the commotion.

Alexander Senior glowered from behind the salesman. He'd claimed to want to come along because he needed to get out of the house, but Alex sincerely wondered if his father was enjoying his predicament.

The salesman pounded his fist against the car frame. "You've come to the right place, Daphne. Your uncle Bob'll fix you right up with the papers if you want her. You ain't gonna get a better price on a car like this anywhere."

Alex groaned.

"It's perfect, Uncle Bob," Daphne breathed. "Don't you think so, Alex? There's enough room to fold a playpen in the back if we need to go somewhere, and for anything else the babies need."

It was so far from perfect that Alex had to grind his teeth to refrain from saying so. Nor was he certain Uncle Bob was the most reputable man he'd ever seen, even for a used-car salesman.

"Not a scratch on her," Uncle Bob said cheerfully. "And not a mile over fifty thousand."

Since the front fender was dented in two places, Alex thought they could safely doubt the veracity of Uncle Bob's word. But he didn't think the Chevy was old enough to have its odometer rolled back. Ostensibly to check the power windows, he pushed a button and put a shield between Daphne and Uncle Bob.

"Honey, maybe we should look at new Suburbans, just for the sake of comparison," he suggested gamely.

"Oh." Daphne's smile slid off her face. "If you think that would be best." But it was clear she was crushed.

Outside, Alexander Senior leaned on his cane as he made a slow circle of the buslike vehicle. Alex's face burned with something he identified as humiliation. With a kingly gesture, his father motioned for Uncle Bob to lift the hood of the car.

"I'd best help Mr. Banning," Sinclair said, getting out.

Nelly and Danita sat silently, each maneuvering a baby. Alex sighed again, closing his eyes. Was it any great revelation that his wife would choose to purchase something to help out a family member? Of course not. Her transportation choice wasn't a big mystery, either. Daphne was no Eliza Doolittle, though perhaps that was how he'd inadvertently treated her by bringing home the limo, good intentions aside. His wife had a couple of advanced degrees in child education and psychology. She had worked her way through college, soaking up the fine arts to the point that she knew a couple of different foreign languages and the names of famous artists and writers to whom he'd only paid cursory attention. She had been a sought-after schoolteacher, loved by parents and children alike for her gentleness and creative approach to teaching. In her spare time, she fashioned beautiful stained-glass artwork, which she sold in boutiques and craft shows. His wife was artsy and unique. He had fallen in love with that aspect of her personality, cherishing her for the fresh air she brought into his rather repressed life.

He should have considered Daphne before he'd bought, instead of basing his decision on what he was used to.

The hood slammed down. His father shrugged at him through the front window, signifying that neither Sinclair nor he saw anything outrageously wrong with the vehicle. Obviously, he didn't see anything good about it, either.

Alex gave a shrug of his own. The truth was, he'd buy a fleet of clunkers from shrewdies named Uncle Bob if it would make Daphne happy. "You're right. It's perfect. Let's drive her home."

"Alex!" Daphne leaned over and kissed him full on the mouth. He savored the hero-of-the-moment feeling her lips on his brought him until Uncle Bob rapped on the window. They pulled away from each other like split hairs as Daphne slid the window down.

"Can I take that to mean I should draw up the papers?" Uncle Bob asked, beaming.

"Yes," Alex replied.

"You're a good girl, Daph," Bob said, leaning in the window to kiss her. "You never forget about your old uncle."

No doubt he was very glad of the extra few thousand dollars he was going to pocket as a result of his niece's purchase, Alex thought sourly as he tugged the rather loose visor down to examine the filmy mirror.

But he'd seen Daphne's face shining with happiness, and as he caught the approving smiles Nelly and Danita wore in the grimy reflection, Alex knew he'd made the right decision.

His father stumped off toward his Mercedes, Sinclair in tow, without saying a word.

"I HAVEN'T given Daphne a present yet," Alexander Banning told Sinclair when they returned home.

The faithful family retainer gently helped his worn-out employer into a chair by the window in his bedroom. "I think she has everything she needs, sir," he said quietly. "Why don't you rest right now?"

"I've got to get her something!" Alexander roared. "How can I not get the woman my son married a gift for her babies? Do you think I like her looking at me like I'm a troll who lives upstairs and may eat her babies the next time I dine?"

"No, sir. Although I believe you're more worried about what Miss Daphne thinks of you than she worries about what you think of her."

"Quit blathering, Sinclair. You're putting static in my hearing aid."

"Yes, sir." Sinclair sighed. "Alex gave her your wife's pearls, but I don't think she's, uh, responded to his gift yet. Er, very well, actually."

Alexander overlooked his employee's bumbling. Sinclair tried too hard, in his opinion. "Of course she didn't receive them with shouts of joy. She's been gone for months, the flighty girl. Why would she care about pearls when there's something else she wants?"

"Oh, sir, I wouldn't suspect Miss Daphne of being a fortune hunter," Sinclair hurried to object.

"Of course she's not! Didn't two hours on a hot, dirty, used-car parking lot with a shiftless member of her family teach you anything?" Alexander shot him a disgruntled frown.

"Um, perhaps not what it should have," Sinclair admitted.

"Ever the politician," Alexander grumbled. "Daphne's not interested in money or position, which makes this damn thing so tricky." He pulled at his chin thoughtfully, staring out the window. "But she is fiercely loyal, which might very well benefit us in the long run."

"Sir?"

"It behooves us to make certain Alex and Daphne stay together for the sake of future sons and for the sake of keeping Green Forks as it is."

Sinclair wrung his hands. "Mr. Banning, if I may say so, perhaps you shouldn't focus on boy heirs so much."

Alexander waved him off. "Of course I should. Oh, I know I seem selfish to you, always harping about boys. But I have to, damn it!" he thundered. "I've spent all morning with my solicitor—oh, never mind," he interrupted himself. "We've got to find a way to help my son's marriage along. How are we going to convince Daphne to move the babies out of her quarters so my son can move in and get to work on baby making? When she's recovered from this birth, of course,'' he added considerately.

Sinclair's face took on a rosy shade, a color Alexander had never seen his unflappable employee wear before.

"Sir," Sinclair whispered, "Nelly tells me that Miss Daphne can't, er, uh—"

"Spit it out, Sinclair! You're too old to develop a speech impediment! You sound like a toddler."

"Yes, sir." Sinclair smoothed his gray hair away from his brow nervously. "Nelly says Miss Daphne can't bear any more children."

"What?" Alexander leaned closer, his heart taking on an abnormal, almost painful rhythm.

"She can't, sir," Sinclair whispered. "I'm sorry."

"Are you positive?"

"The odds do not appear to be in her favor, short of a miracle."

Alexander slowly leaned back and stared out the window, seeing the rolling hills of the land he loved and the steers grazing contentedly. It was a comfortably breezy, sun-filled day, yet shock and disappointment fed the fear inside him. Fear and overwhelming concern.

Alexander took a heavy breath, which wedged in his chest like a blacksmith's iron. "It's over, then."

"Sir?"

"It doesn't matter anymore." He waved his trusted butler away and allowed his hand to drop limply onto the chair. He sat silently for a few moments as he mulled over the past, and the future, and what he couldn't keep from slipping from his once-powerful hands. "I love my son, you know."

"Yes, sir."

"We've never had a particularly easy relation-ship."

"No, sir," Sinclair agreed.

Alexander rubbed his head, slightly nettled by his butler's honesty. "I've been grateful for the second chance." He thought for a moment, sighing deeply. "I should tell him, I suppose," he said, almost to himself. "Truth is, if Alex had to choose between this ranch and Daphne, he'd choose his woman."

"Of course, sir. He would be like his father in that regard. Only one woman to hold his heart."

"Hmph." Alexander tried not to look wistful as he thought of his deceased Sabrina. It was true, though. There had only been one woman, one woman alone, who had captured his heart and kept it. "Ah, well," he muttered, defeated. "I've done my best. It would just stir up trouble if I tell him."

"Sir?"

He pursed his lips, ignoring his employee's con-fusion. As long as he had breath in his body, he would do everything he could to hold his family together. "I can still give my daughter-in-law a gift she'll like, though. Sinclair, take me to the store."

"Do you know what you're after, sir?"

"Have you ever known me not to know my own mind?" he loudly demanded, just to show that he still had everything under control. Only he knew he didn't.

And it was all because of those pink-beribboned granddaughters of his.

Chapter Six

The problem, as best Alex could discern, was that Daphne, being naturally independent, was more than capable of being a single parent. He knew she still loved him, despite the fact she had left their marriage. It was a temporary setback he chose to overcome. His entire lineage of paternal Bannings was made up of men who overcame setbacks to become great men. One petite, adorably fiery woman shouldn't prove too great a resistance to the success of his marriage— particularly since he knew she loved him. And, though she proclaimed it to be a transient situation, she was in his home, on his turf.

The complex angle was discovering how to win her. He wasn't arrogant enough to believe that buying questionable vehicles from her family members was enough to win Daphne's heart. His mother's pearls hadn't appeared to warm her toward him, either. She couldn't be bought, an unworthy tactic his father had worked on Daphne's father, Cos. No, there had to be something more that would convince her that they belonged together.

He just couldn't put his finger on what that was,

when he'd thought all along love would be enough between them. When had that changed?

It really made his chest hurt to think they simply might be too dissimilar. If Daphne wasn't happy being in the same house with him and the children, maybe their marriage wasn't going to work. After all, it took two people to make a marriage, and as Daphne had said many times, she wanted a divorce. The days were ticking slowly toward their anniversary.

He didn't think he could face it. Yet it was the only thing she seemed to want from him.

Sighing, he decided to pay his father a visit. Maybe Alexander, a strategist in his own right, could tell him where he was erring in his pursuit of the woman he loved. Rounding the corner, he stopped at the sound of Daphne's voice.

She was talking to the babies on the stair landing, holding one of his offspring as she looked at the portraits of the Banning ancestors.

"And this is the second Alexander," she said softly to the baby in her arms. The other two babies lay in the triple stroller, apparently paying great attention to the singsong notes of Daphne's voice, though Alex doubted they were absorbing their genealogy lesson.

"Oh, don't cry, angel," Daphne told the baby.

From his narrow vantage point, it appeared she was addressing Alex Junior.

"Oh, that was just a hiccup. I see. I was afraid you were concerned by Alexander the Second's stern visage. I assure you that, while all of the men in this family wear those frowns, they are nothing to be frightened of," she cooed to the baby.

Alex's jaw dropped. He didn't have stern features!

"What's that, Miss Magoo? Why are there no maternal ancestral portraits? That's a very good question," Daphne answered. "It's because no one has suggested it yet. Now that you have, we must investigate the possibility. Because for every great man, there's a great female to whom he owes his success in one form or another."

Alex held back a chuckle even as he thought through Daphne's statement. Why *were* there no portraits of women lining the staircase? It was true, what Daphne said. His mother had been his father's greatest asset.

"You're right, Yoda. As we all know, male and female children have the same degree of potential. This ancestor, for example, Alexander the Third, understood that very well. You can see on his brass plate that he was a world-renowned chef. This was an illustrious achievement, because he created meals of such wonder that he was sought after by royalty and heads of state. However, if you would pay closer attention to the nameplate than your bib, Miss Magoo, you will see that he also cooked at local soup kitchens on Sundays. Quite progressive, even for a Banning male, wouldn't you say?"

Alex shook his head as the history lesson ended on a wail from one of the babies. He walked up the staircase. Daphne held one baby to her and pushed the triple stroller with the other hand to the elevator.

"Let me get that," he said as the doors slid open.

Daphne smiled briefly at him. "Thanks. The girls just decided they were hungry."

"I see they like their new stroller." Two of his daughters lay inside the contraption, looking at him with wondering eyes. They were probably mesmerized by the elevator lights, but all the same, he liked thinking they recognized him.

"Yes. The stroller was an ingenious gift from my parents. I really appreciate it." She patted the handles happily. "It's the only way I can get all three infants around at the same time. I feel like I'm spending family time with them, instead of shuffling them around like wrapped bundles."

He smiled, even though he felt a little left out. When the elevator doors opened on the first floor, he made certain they stayed open long enough for Daphne to move the triple stroller past them, but she didn't even look at him.

"Thank you," she said, pushing the babies down the hallway toward her room.

It *was* her room. Indecisively, he wondered if she wanted him with her. She certainly hadn't said, and she hadn't shown any great happiness that he'd joined her. She disappeared inside her quarters without a word to him, no invitation to join her in the feeding frenzy his babies were demanding.

There had to be a way to win his woman back. He had everything a man usually needed to get the woman of his dreams—wealth and position, chiefly.

None of it was doing him a bit of good.

Then the lightbulb went on. He saw the logical battle plan. Daphne believed in equal rights, equal opportunities. That's the lesson she'd been teaching her daughters during the family tree lecture. Therefore, she couldn't shut him out from his family. He had equal rights, too!

And he could be a great father. Not autocratic and austere, like his father had been during Alex's childhood. He'd win her heart with a devoted dad demonstration.

Purposefully, Alex strode to Daphne's quarters. One baby slept, one cried in Danita's arms and one nursed at Daphne's breast, a sight that fascinated Alex and sent hot desire searing through him.

"Danita, I'll take that one," he said, reaching for the crying baby. Anything to get his mind off Daphne's sexy, nicely rounded breasts!

"Okay." Danita relinquished her charge and rose. "I'll head down to the kitchen and fix Daphne some lunch."

"That's all right, Mother. You don't have to go," Daphne protested, but Mrs. Way made the fastest exit Alex had ever seen. Without appearing too pleased, he commandeered the rocker and began to comfort his daughter.

Daphne scowled at him as she covered her breasts. Alex smiled at her pleasantly.

"What are you up to?" she demanded.

"Holding my daughter," he said innocently. "You need help with these babies. I'm going to help you."

"I want my mother," she insisted.

"As a father, I find it incumbent to execute my paternal duties." He gave her his politician's smile, the one he used when locked into battle with fierce opponents.

"Incumbent?"

"Necessary," he supplied.

"I know what it means," she snapped. "I'm asking you why you suddenly feel this way."

"It's not sudden. I want to be with you and the children."

She was silent for a moment. The blouse parted, revealing what she'd tried to hide from him. He tried not to stare at his baby nursing at Daphne's breast. Something told him if he looked in that direction he would activate his wife's alarm system. Despite the fact that the smooth, pale globe of flesh tugged at his vision with an undeniable need to stare, he forced himself to meet Daphne's green eyes.

"You tried to get me to move them into the nursery!"

"Yes, well, that was so you could get some rest," he replied smoothly. "But I think we could all sleep together just fine until they're older."

"We're not sleeping together at all," she said tightly. "Alex, if this is because of the car you bought me—"

"It's not!" he denied hastily. "The car is yours without any obligation. I only want to make your life easier."

"By sleeping with me? That won't make my life easier!"

"I could help you with the babies in the night."

"My mother is just fine," she insisted.

Maybe he could convince Mrs. Way to move home. Alex rapidly reviewed that scenario.

"My mother has assured me she'll stay as long as I need her."

His surprised gaze jumped to her indignant one. So his little wife was a mind reader, as well. And obviously quite determined to thwart him at every chance. Staring at her jutting chin, Alex reconsidered his game plan.

They handed off babies a few silent minutes later, brushing hands as they did so. The contact sent Alex's focus clean off his strategizing. Daphne's exposed nipple shot the rest of his concentration.

"I just want you to give me a chance to be a good father and husband," he stated, forgetting all about slick maneuvers.

"Okay." The mulish set to her jaw eased a bit. "How are you going to do that?"

"I don't know!" He gave her an impatient stare. "But I'm willing to learn."

"Hmm." She appeared to consider his words. "It's not my intention to keep you away from your children. I'm sorry if I've given you that impression. I honestly assumed you would be more comfortable with the staff taking care of the babies."

"I...may have thought that in the beginning," he said slowly, sensing he was gaining an advantage but confused as to how to capitalize on it. "But I think it's the only way to win your heart," he finished honestly, not knowing if he'd just annihilated his position.

Daphne sat nursing for a moment, her eyes locked with Alex's. "You were not a bad husband," she finally said, her tone soft and reluctant. "You made me very happy."

"Then what the hell happened?" The baby in his

arms started at his tone, blinking at him. He wrapped its blanket around it more securely and met Daphne's gaze again.

Daphne pursed her lips. She couldn't tell him what had happened! If she admitted she'd heard his death-bed promise to his father to have male children, Alex would say that wasn't important to him.

It was important to her, all the more so since Alexander had bought her father's runty cattle at a highly elevated price. She'd seen the look on Alexander's face yesterday when his son had bought the Suburban from Uncle Bob. In his mind, the used-car salesman had been out to make easy bucks off him, like Cos had made easy bucks off Alexander. No doubt he wondered how much more money he was going to have to give the Way family before he got a return on his investment.

"What happened," she said slowly, "was that I just decided I couldn't live with you anymore."

"Well, I'm going to change your mind." His voice was steady with promise and determination.

You don't have to change my mind! She'd never wanted to be away from Alex before the babies had been born. It had been sheer torture to keep him at a distance when she'd really wanted him to hold her and reassure her in the night.

She had to disturb Alex's serious intentions. There was more to their problem than could be fixed at this stage in the game. "Don't worry about changing my mind. Change Miss Magoo's T-shirt," she instructed, "and put her down for her nap."

He stared at the baby in his arms. "Change her T-shirt?"

"Yes. It has milk on it. Would *you* like to sleep in a wet shirt?" She forced her voice to be no-nonsense as she finished with Yoda's feeding and began to work a burp out of her.

"No, I wouldn't." He looked at the baby doubtfully. "But I don't want to change her shirt. Let me burp that one, and you change this one."

"No. Yoda is hard to burp."

The baby let out a noise that sounded like a bottle rocket had been set off.

"Good girl," Daphne praised. "Now I'll freshen up your diaper. The shirt, Alex, and then the diaper."

She could see his reluctance as he laid his daughter on the bed.

"I'm afraid I'm going to pull one of her arms off, or a finger." He gave the baby an uneasy look.

"Trust me, she won't break. Just be gentle."

She walked over to watch him carefully take off the tiny white shirt. The baby appeared more interested in yawning than her father's trauma at undressing her. Alex swiftly changed the diaper, put a fresh T-shirt on and wrapped the baby in a pink blanket, sending Daphne an exultant smile.

"There!"

He looked so proud of himself she had to smile.

"Give me that one. I'm on a roll here! You know, this diaper-changing stuff is a piece of cake. If one approaches it from a business perspective, diapers are basically...well, paper and tape. I think I'm going to be pretty good at this." His tone triumphant, he reached for the baby she held, determined to duplicate his victory. Bemused, she allowed him to take the baby from her.

The sound of another bottle rocket firing startled both of them. Spit-up ran down the front of Alex's well-pressed, expensive shirt.

"Oh, dear!" Daphne started to reach for the baby but instantly stopped herself. Alex had said he wanted to be a father to his children. Sometimes it was a messy, stinky job. "You'll have to bathe her now."

"Bathe *her! I* need a bath." He glared at the baby, who began wailing, and then at Daphne, who felt like joining the little one. But she pointed at the infant bathtub. Ignoring his pleading expression, she sat down to feed a quiet Alex Junior a bottle.

"I can do that," Alex offered too quickly.

"No, thanks." Daphne shook her head at him. "Don't be scared of one tiny baby and a bit of water."

"It's not water, it's throw-up!"

"I meant, put a bit of water in the bathtub and be brave about it."

"What if I hurt her?"

"You won't. As you have pointed out, you always knew how to wash me very well. It's one of your talents."

With that, she left the room, carrying Alex Junior in her arms.

She had to. It was too easy to want to get into the shower with Alex after the babies were snug in their cribs and allow him to hold her. It was a temptation she couldn't allow herself to endure.

But she stayed in the hall listening to Alex murmur to his daughter in the same gentle voice he'd always used with her, and her heart filled to bursting with unhappiness that they couldn't go back to the way they'd been before.

AT THE FORMAL dinner table that night, Alex, Danita, Daphne and Alexander ate quietly. Though the afternoon had finished much more leisurely than it had begun, despite the round of feeding, changing and bathing the babies required, Alex felt he'd made headway. He was tired but proud. Daphne appeared to have softened somewhat toward him. He would gladly endure ten years of the same routine he'd suffered this afternoon if it meant his wife would want him. He knew that, Herculean as raising children might be, even more than that was required to win his wife's heart again.

"Mr. Banning," Sinclair said in his most formal butler tone, "Mr. Way is here to see his daughter and wife. And grandchildren," Sinclair added, in a pompous afterthought.

The quiet, worn-out atmosphere in the room instantly charged. Daphne's gaze darted to his. At the head of the table Alexander sat straight, braced as if enemies were approaching his stronghold.

"Howdy, neighbors and family members," Cos said too cheerfully as he seated himself at the table without being asked. "I see I dropped in at a good time."

He hadn't bothered to kiss his daughter or wife, Alex noticed with a frown. Without waiting to be served, Cos reached to take a bowl from the sideboard behind him as Sinclair hurriedly placed a plate and silver in front of him. Obviously, with Danita gone, he'd missed home-cooked meals.

Daphne rose and walked around the table to her father, then gave him a brief hug. "Hello, Father."

"Hello, honey," he said, glancing up from the generous helping of meat Sinclair was ladling onto his plate. "Where're my grandbabies, sugar?"

He emphasized "my" too much, Alex realized. Suddenly, he knew that Cos felt left out. He was as uncomfortable as everyone else at the table and trying desperately to fit in. For Daphne's sake, Alex reminded himself to be courteous.

"Napping," Daphne answered.

"When they wake up, we'll make sure you get an introduction," Alex said. The grateful look Daphne sent him was worth the effort.

"Need to tell your daughter to come up with decent names for those babies, Cos!" Alexander thundered from the head of the table.

"Decent?" Cos puffed up. "I'm sure any names my daughter has chosen are just fine!"

The ongoing feud was about to flare. Alex started to try to douse it, but Daphne's voice stopped him.

"Actually, I haven't named them yet. I mean, Alex and I haven't," she said guiltily.

"Why not?" Cos stared at his daughter.

"We…haven't discussed it yet." She sent Alex a shamed glance. He reached to cover her hand with his own.

"What in blazes have you been doing, girlie?"

"We, ah—" Daphne faltered.

"We've been getting settled in." Alex squeezed her hand.

"They'll name 'em when they're ready, Cos," Danita interrupted. "Eat your potatoes and mind your own business." She leaned over and gave him a dry peck on the cheek to take the sting out of her words, so Cos dug into his food like he hadn't seen any in days.

Alex wondered if he had. Now that he was taking an active hand in helping his wife, maybe Danita could go home. He brightened at that idea. Although he wouldn't have said so before Cos's unexpected entrance, perhaps his arrival was a good thing. He slid an assessing look at his wife. She had her long bronze hair up in a turquoise ribbon, which shone in the candlelight. A turquoise maternity outfit looked comfortable on her, clinging gently to her body. He'd get her some new clothes when she felt like shopping. She'd probably enjoy an outing at the mall. They could stroll the babies—

"Damn cows you sold me ain't worth the hair on their skinny hides!" Alexander erupted.

"They are!" Cos dropped his fork, stung. A bit of gravy dribbled onto his shirtfront. "You just gotta give 'em a chance!"

"Well, they eat like pigs. Maybe you sold me pigs in steers' clothing." Alexander peered the length of the table at Cos. "I think I got swindled. They look like you when they eat, like they've never seen food."

Alex stared at Daphne over the flickering candles,

seeing the hope in her eyes wane. Alexander glowered like a regal warrior king at his worthless subject. Cos stared back mutinously.

The feud was on.

Chapter Seven

"Quit yer crankin', Alexander," Cos instructed. "It must be true that the rich stay rich 'cause they don't let a penny out of their sight. If you'd feed those steers properly, they'd grow. Hope you're feeding my daughter better. As a matter of fact, you're looking pale yerself. Best stick yer head into yer own feed bag." He picked up his fork and resumed eating, ignoring his host's wrathful expression.

"I have fed those steers properly! They're just rangy, bottomless skin bags."

"Healthy. Make it through another drought, if we have another." He glanced at Alexander. "Listen, you stingy old man, are you gonna eat or argue all night? I'm hungry."

"I can see that."

"Well, heck fire! You got the best of all I got here at Green Forks, Alexander. You got my cattle, you got my wife and you got my daughter. Heard you even been over to see my brother Bob to bleed him outta the best car he had on the lot. Bob cain't feed his family on the profit he made on that Chevy."

"I had nothing to do with that!" Alexander sent

his son an inquiring look. "Alex paid for the car. Full price, inflated enough to send your brother to Tahiti for a week, I imagine."

"Actually, I did negotiate a bit," Alex interjected uncomfortably. "The car seemed a bit overpriced."

"Man, the apple don't fall far from the tree, does it?" Cos said to no one in particular.

Alex met Daphne's astonished gaze over the crystal candelabrum. Surely she didn't believe the claptrap her father was peddling?

"My poor brother Bob," Cos said around a mouthful of prime rib. "And him with eight children."

"All boys," Alexander intoned.

"Yep. Every one of 'em," Cos agreed cheerfully.

Alexander bowed his head. "Well, at least I don't have to feed *them*," he murmured. Glancing up, he caught Alex's stern gaze on him. Alex raised his eyebrows meaningfully at his father, hoping he'd get the point to give quarter. The contrast between the two men was stark. Cos had nothing. A wife, many children—grown men—and a piece of land that bordered on poverty. Alexander had no wife, one son and an enormous spread that could only be called palatial.

Cos was the richer man. Apparently, that fact nagged at Alexander like a broken spur.

Everyone waited tensely for the next barb to be shot from the patriarch's bow.

"Of course," Alexander said slowly, his gaze moving to his daughter-in-law's pale face, "since part of your family is here, you should have brought your boys, Cos. I'm sure they'd enjoy seeing their new nieces.'' He glanced at Alex, his expression slightly ashamed.

''Well, why didn't you say so!'' Cos leaped to his feet. ''They're all just hanging around waiting for an invite. I'll give 'em a call.''

Alex grinned at his father's grunt. He wondered if his father suspected just how easily he'd been maneuvered into feeding the entire Way family. Still, it wouldn't hurt anything, and it might please Daphne. She sat watching him, her face still and slightly worried.

''Haven't told you yet that some ranchers from Chile are interested in those worthless hairy beasts you sold me,'' Alexander said conversationally before Cos could make the phone call.

The entire group looked at Alexander.

''Ranchers from Chile?'' Cos repeated, sitting down.

Alex thought his father looked just a bit too smug.

Alexander picked up a crystal wineglass, taking his time, drawing out his announcement. ''Apparently, they saw a couple of them at the stock show. They'd like to crossbreed them.'' He took a long drink of wine. ''Be some good profit in that.''

Cos's knife clattered to his plate. ''The stock show was before your son married my daughter and got her pregnant!''

''All this talk of impregnation is turning my appetite.'' Danita tried to interrupt.

Alexander didn't reply. The hair on the back of Alex's neck electrified. Daphne kicked him under the table and jerked her head at his father.

As if I could forcibly remove him from the middle of a battle, Alex thought in disgust.

"You bought those cattle from me knowing they were going to be worth a lotta money!" Cos protested. "You sneaky thief!"

"You wanted to sell me those starved creatures because they weren't worth a dog's bald ear on the auction block," Alexander asserted. "Look like toothpicks holding up hairbrushes."

"That's what the Chileans want them for! They sees they're hardy. You tricked me!"

"Now, Cos." Alexander held up a hand, clearly delighted to have gotten the upper hand. "You were trying to cheat me, and I just cheated you better."

Daphne jumped to her feet and threw her napkin onto the table. With an angry glare at every person present, she excused herself and left the room.

"YOUR FATHER is incorrigible!" Daphne yelled at Alex as soon as he breached the threshold of her room. "He deliberately tries to keep my father in his place!"

Unfortunately, he had to agree with her.

"All this talk of who bested who is despicable! And your father loves it!" She curled her hands onto her hips.

"Honey, I think your dad was enjoying it a little until he realized he'd been outmaneuvered."

"Outmaneuvered! That's like comparing a toy soldier to a hydrogen bomb, Alex. One is harmless, the other is a weapon!"

From the rocking chair, Nelly gave a loud shush.

"Okay, okay," he said to Daphne. "I'll mention to my father that he needs to go a little easier on Cos." He held up his hands in surrender, then put a finger to his lips. The last thing he wanted was babies waking, but he had to calm his irate wife. Although there were some family loyalties involved, he did tend to agree with her. But Cos Way irritated the devil out of his father, and that was a fact nobody was going to change. Alexander lived to best the farmer, and that was the nature of their relationship. Couldn't Daphne see how old and frail his father was? Didn't she understand the game Cos and Alexander had been playing for decades was relatively harmless—until her father always cried foul?

"Money, money, money! Why does everything have to come back to money?" Daphne stormed. Whirling on him, she gave him a narrow look. "And did you really hardball Uncle Bob on the price of the Chevy?"

"Well…" He scratched the back of his neck. He'd been buying a car, for heaven's sake! Didn't she expect some haggling? "Of course I negotiated for a better price, hon. There's always some cushion built into—"

"That's what's wrong with you and your father, Alex! You'd pinch every penny in your pocket till it screamed before paying for a used Chevy for me, but you'd pay fifteen times as much for a chauffeured Rolls with bulletproof glass."

"Shh." Alex glanced at the sleeping babies. Nelly stared at both of them before glancing worriedly at her charges.

There was no way they could talk in here. Alex pulled his wife by the hand down the hall. They crept along a narrow hallway, past the formal area, and hurried outside. A gazebo on the front lawn beckoned Alex, and he dragged a reluctant Daphne toward it.

When they reached the white-painted building, he tugged Daphne inside and pulled her down beside him. "I'm sorry I cut into Uncle Bob's profit. If it will make you feel any better, I haggled like hell on the price of the Rolls. I must have some of my old man in me." Unable to wait any longer and not wanting to argue at all, he covered her lips with his and kissed her. She struggled half a second before she wound her hands into his hair and returned his kisses.

"This isn't going to solve anything," she murmured against his mouth as they both took a breath.

"I know, but I've been wanting to kiss you since you got here. Give a guy a break."

"I don't feel sorry for you at all. You think you can just drag me off and have your way with me like any old conqueror."

"Well, isn't being dragged off better than listening to them debate who's gotten one up on whom?" He sneaked a hand inside her floaty blouse and rubbed her back.

"It might be," she said, swiftly catching his hand before he could undo her bra clasp, "but they are the root of our problems."

"Let's forget about our roots and focus on our tree instead, Daph," he pleaded, pressing his face between her breasts. She held him tightly to her, and Alex could hear her thundering heartbeat. "We're growing some great branches. I'd like to be happy about that."

"I don't know if we can." Reluctantly, she slid out of his lap and sat on the plank beside him. "Your father really believes my father is a dishonest peddler."

"And your father believes mine is a cheap son of a gun. Who cares what they think about each other?" He put his arm around her, pulling her close. "Look at the stars, Daphne. There's so much out there, and this is a big ranch. We can get away from our folks any time we need to."

"No, we can't. They're part of us, who we are. And we're just kidding ourselves if we think any differently."

She looked so sad that Alex wanted to cry. "I refuse to believe that I'm my father or that you are yours."

"You don't understand how bad it makes me feel to know that you were willing to pay for a fine car but you turned cheapskate on a used car that cost pocket change to you. I feel like that in our relationship."

"Daph, I would spare no expense to make you happy," he said in surprise.

"No, I meant that…I don't know what I meant. I guess I feel undervalued because I'm a Way." Her brows crept toward her forehead.

"Well, don't, for God's sake." He kissed her neck and moved slowly down to her fingertips before holding them to his mouth. "You are all I want."

"I haven't kept my value up. There isn't any way

I'm going to turn out prizewinning cattle like the ones my father sold your dad. There isn't going to be a profit on your investment this time.''

"Hush, Daph." He pulled her other hand to his mouth to kiss each of the fingertips slowly. How could he tell this woman that, regardless of how it looked to her, she had his father's bent for financial control confused with his need for her love? "Let's do something very simple to prove how reasonable and levelheaded we are when our parents aren't playing Hatfield and McCoy."

"Okay. I can be reasonable and levelheaded." But her tone was reluctant.

"Let's name the children."

"That's a minefield!"

"No, it's not. That's my point." He pulled his recalcitrant wife into his lap. "Watch how well we do this. You start."

"Well, I was thinking Sabrina Caroline, after your mother, would be nice for Yoda," she slowly said. "She's going to be beautiful when she grows lashes," Daphne assured him.

"Sabrina Caroline. A lovely choice." To disguise how touched he was, Alex began nibbling on her neck. She sighed, leaning her head back, and he couldn't keep from moving his hands under her shirt to cup her breasts.

"And I thought," Daphne continued dreamily, "we could name Miss Magoo after my mother."

"Danita?" Alex's hands stilled, his pulse slowing a bit. He wouldn't have said it, but that wasn't a name he would have chosen. Still, he reminded himself to keep his mouth shut.

"My mother's name is Danielle," Daphne told him huffily. "Dad calls her Danita, but that's just a nickname."

"Oh," he said on a relieved breath. "I like Danielle." He closed his eyes and braved reaching under her bra.

"Danielle Cos."

"What?" His hands stopped short of their goal.

"See? You don't like my father's name! But I have to include him somehow."

Alex looked into Daphne's hurt gaze. "I like Cos. Just not for a girl."

"What's wrong with Danielle Cos Banning?" she demanded frostily. "Lots of girls bear a family name."

"Well, we don't want our daughter bearing too much." He switched his hands to Daphne's back and began massaging, sensing that she was too wary for the kind of caresses he had in mind. "How about we compromise? Danielle Constance Banning. That's close to Cos."

Daphne straightened, her bottom shifting nicely against his erection. "I think I like that."

"I know I do," he said with a groan. Thank heavens they had one more child to name! Reaching for her delicate hips, he moved her against him ever so gently.

"Okay. That leaves Alex Junior."

"Go for it." He wasn't paying a bit of attention to naming babies anymore. His mind was solely occupied by the feel of Daphne in his lap, and how much he wanted her.

"Alexis Abigail Banning," she pronounced.

"Abigail?" he repeated, his concentration momentarily arrested despite his wish to be focused on nothing but Daphne.

"Alexis for you," she murmured into his ear as she rested against his shoulder.

"Because she's the ugly one," he rejoined. "You've got your father in you, Daphne Way." But he loved the tickling feel of her breath in his ear. "But Abigail?"

"I saw it in a baby book. In Hebrew, it means 'father is rejoicing.'" Purposefully, she turned, shifting against his erection as she put her arms around his neck.

"I know I am," he said, burying his face in her breasts. "See how wonderfully we work together?"

"Yes." Daphne said on a breathy sigh. "If I could, I would make love with you right now, Alex. But it's a few more weeks until I can have intercourse."

He raised his head and looked at her. "I can think of other ways to make you happy."

"I can think of some ways to make you happy, too." She gave him a tantalizing smile and reached for his zipper.

He groaned. "Promise me you're not going to leave after our anniversary, Daphne." But he allowed her to entice him onto the floor of the gazebo. Overhead, the stars twinkled with light and faraway magic.

"I don't want to make any promises right now."

Her hands slid away from him. "You said I could have the time before our anniversary to decide."

Alex recaptured her hands and put them back on his groin. He reached under the elastic of her maternity pants to fondle her buttocks, then slid his palms lower.

Right now, he was willing to give on the promises if Daphne would keep doing what she was doing. And maybe loving her the way he wanted to would make her realize how much they needed each other.

"We still have to get through the christenings," she softly reminded him. "And our families can't even sit through a casual dinner together."

"So? It's a little water, a few pictures. What could go wrong with that? Piece of cake. Mm, you're delicious." He nibbled her neck, which made her giggle softly and arch against him. In the quiet, they loved each other until they climaxed, united in pleasured sharing they both craved.

For a few moments, Daphne relaxed against Alex and looked at the stars. A slight evening breeze blew across them, bringing the scent of grass and farmland.

We really could be in heaven, she thought wistfully, *if only everything was different.*

BY THE TIME Alex and Daphne returned, the feuding families were seated in the enormous den comforting babies, which seemed to take precedence over bickering. Guiltily, Daphne flew to take the loudest noisemaker from Nelly. "I'm so sorry! I forgot about the time."

"Relax, honey. They hadn't let out a peep until just now. Think they heard you coming."

Danita nodded. "Besides, if we'd had to, we coulda tided them over with a water bottle."

Alex helped her pack the babies into the stroller. A trifle nervously—could they tell she and Alex had been recovering some of their marital joy?—she glanced around the room. Alexander had a blanket over his lap as if he were cold on this summer day. Cos was seated near Alexander. Danita sat across the room. Somehow, they looked peaceful, as if they'd all been enjoying a cup of after dinner coffee.

Maybe Alex was right. Maybe it was a situation her parents were used to—one her father even got a little enjoyment out of. Still, she wouldn't want to spend her life trying to best Alexander.

Or his son. Alex was far too determined, like her father. Nudging his hand away from the stroller, which he clearly intended to push to her quarters, Daphne moved down the hall. "I'll be back shortly," she told the assembled group. "Alex, you stay with your dad and hold down the fort."

His brows went up. "Don't you need help?"

"My mom can help me," she answered, wheeling faster. She had to get away from Alex just for a little while. She couldn't believe how easily she'd succumbed to his arms. The truth was, she wasn't keeping her resolve very well. Maybe her struggle was pointless. Maybe it didn't matter how she felt about being swapped for several hundred puny cattle. They'd turned out to be valuable.

She hadn't. Not the way Alexander had hoped.

But Alexander seemed happy with her, as happy as he ever seemed with anything. Or was that just a front for Alex's sake? The way Alexander dug at her father made her feel there was some lingering resentment between the families.

Maybe she and Alex were the answer, though. Their marriage could cement the two houses. After all, what did she and Alex care if their parents kept up a feud? Kind of hard to do with three little grand-daughters running across the road and between farms.

She reached her room and sank into the rocker, swiftly holding one baby to her while Danita picked up another. Alexis Abigail lay quietly waiting her turn, as usual.

Supposedly Alexander had changed his will, Daphne mused. What did that mean? Surely he meant to include her children, even though they weren't the sex he'd wanted? Until tonight, he'd seemed angry about something. Angry about her, about the children, she'd thought. Certainly, he hadn't been pleased with her choice of vehicle. But the crusty old man hadn't made any overt sign of disgust, either, and she hadn't known him to be tacit about his opinions in the past.

She'd ask him how he felt about her and the children. It was the only logical thing to do. Especially if she wanted her marriage to make it past the one-year mark. Alex didn't seem to be suffering from any lack of commitment to their vows.

She was the one who felt like she wasn't worth a "dog's bald ear on the auction block," as Alexander had so strongly put it. Since every discussion in this family revolved around dollars and cents, she was going to determine her value as the patriarch of the family saw it.

And put her mind at ease.

Chapter Eight

When she returned to the family room half an hour later, everyone was watching an old film. A young version of Alexander rode hell-bent for leather over Green Forks land. Daphne squinted at the screen and took a seat next to Alex. His father had been so young and so handsome in his day! So much like Alex. He picked up her hand and held it in his, and Daphne didn't have the heart to pull away. All she could think of was how old Alexander looked now. His recent bout of ill health was something she'd thought he'd gotten over. He was the strong oak tree at Green Forks, a vital landmark she couldn't imagine withering with time.

As she glanced at him, his frail shoulders quivered as he coughed. The image of his youth flashed on the screen, waving a hat and herding cattle. Daphne lowered her eyes. It was too painful to see the contrast.

The tape ended a minute later and the lights were turned up.

"We decided to look at Green Forks a while back," Alexander told her.

"About a hunnerd years ago," Cos joked.

"Hundred my foot. Even the movie projector isn't that old." But Alexander grinned. "I could still ride a horse like that if I was of a mind to."

"Of course you could," Cos agreed. "And so could I."

Everyone in the room laughed. Cos couldn't ride a horse at all, could barely stay in the saddle. Alexander used to love to gibe at him about being the dude rancher. But Cos had managed to keep up what he'd felt was most important—raising his family. And his sons had all learned to ride and rodeo with the best of them.

Alexander took a long drink from his coffee mug before handing it to Sinclair. "I've got a little something I want to give to Daphne," he announced.

Her lips parted as she somewhat suspiciously watched Sinclair hand Alexander a large white bag. What did he have up his sleeve now? Uncertainly, she glanced at Alex, but he shrugged. Apparently, his father was a mystery to him, as well.

"I hope you won't think I've been presumptuous, Daphne," Alexander began, "considering you haven't even properly tagged those young 'uns of yours." He paused to let his point sink in.

"Oh, but I have!" she rejoined, delighted to be able to spring that on the cagey old man. So this was how her father felt when matching wits with Alexander. It was kind of fun to be one step ahead of him. Smiling, she said, "Alex and I discussed it tonight."

"And?" Alexander demanded.

Everyone in the room waited breathlessly. Daphne hugged the knowledge to her for one second longer.

Alex squeezed her fingers lightly. She glanced at him. He was wearing the same huge grin she could feel on her own lips. "Shall I tell them?"

"It would be cruel to make them wait." He nodded. "Go ahead."

"I meant, should I tell them or do you want to?"

"The pleasure is all yours." His eyes sparkled at her.

"I'm enjoying keeping your father in suspense," she said loudly so Alexander could hear.

"Hmph!" Alexander retorted. "Spit it out, Daphne Way. I'm not going to be around forever, you know. And the least you can do is let me go to my grave satisfied that you've finally named those granddaughters of mine something that won't embarrass them."

She drew herself up. "I take that to mean you aren't fond of their current names." But she gave him a wicked smile. "The one I have been calling Yoda is named Sabrina Caroline."

The tears that jumped into Alexander's eyes were no surprise to her. A moment's joy filled her at his happiness.

"Good enough," he said gruffly.

She glanced at Alex with delight. "And Miss Magoo is now Danielle Constance. Danielle for Mom and Constance for Dad."

Cos got up and crossed to hug his wife, apparently more emotional than Alexander was capable of being.

"And last, but never, never least in any way, Alex Junior—" Daphne paused with a luminous look at her husband "—will be named Alexis Abigail."

Everyone clapped except Alexander.

"Where'd Abigail come from?" he demanded.

"It's Hebrew, Dad," Alex told him.

"No Hebrews in this family," Alexander said, honestly perplexed.

Alex laughed. "It means, 'Father is rejoicing.'"

"Hmph." Alexander sat still for a moment, digesting that information. He adjusted his lap robe and cleared his throat. "Well. I guess I am, at that. Well done, Daphne Way."

Alex gave her a swift kiss. Daphne beamed with pride. It didn't matter that Alex was the father who was rejoicing. If Alexander was, too, then that pleased her all the more.

"Can I give you this now?" Alexander pointed to the bag in his lap. "I'd like to get it out of the way before I get any older."

She went to sit beside him. "By all means."

From the bag he pulled a box wrapped in white with a blue-flowered ribbon on top. It was light and barely rustled when she shook it.

"Something to hang from the mirror in my Chevy?" she guessed.

"Open it, girl."

So she did, pulling out the most beautiful white baby gown she'd ever seen. "Oh, my," she breathed, holding it up. "It's lovely." Small scrolls of lace and appliquéd satin decorated the tiny bodice before falling into a sweeping skirt long enough to cover baby toes. "Wherever did you find it, Alexander?"

He appeared inordinately pleased with himself. "In an antique shop."

"Did you really?" She glanced at him, delighted beyond anything she could express.

"I did." He nodded. "I figured only something original and one-of-a-kind would suit my daughter-in-law." He reached into the bag and handed her another white-wrapped box, this one with a pink-flowered ribbon.

Her fingers trembling, she took it from him. Another white christening gown lay inside, with delicate ducks-and-chicks smocking. Daphne felt tears coming to her eyes. "It's beautiful."

"Fortunately for me, those ladies up in town knew exactly which shops had christening gowns," he said with a stern look at Daphne, which she knew covered his emotions. "Otherwise, I might have had to go to Neiman Marcus for these bits of lace. That would have cost me an arm and a leg."

She laughed, not fooled by his attempt to disguise his feelings. "Something tells me these gowns wouldn't have been any more expensive at Neiman Marcus." Taking the last box he handed her, this one wrapped in white with a silver-flowered bow, Daphne said, "You almost had me believing your act, Alexander."

"Don't get too sure of yourself, missy."

Smiling, she drew out the last gown, the best of all. It had lace forget-me-nots scattered down the skirt and the tiniest silver threads she'd ever seen woven into daisy trails across the bodice. Full-lace cap sleeves gave the gown an old-world, fairy-tale appearance. "Oh, Alexander." It was all she could say. She threw her arms around his neck.

"Here! Here!" he cried, making no move to disentangle himself. "Don't suffocate me!"

She felt a warm, dry peck on her cheek, and as Daphne kissed the top of Alexander's head, tears of happiness streamed down her cheeks.

THEY DECIDED to have the christening two days later. It was when the minister was first available, and Daphne felt some urgency, though she couldn't say why. She only knew it was important they not wait another moment. For some reason, and maybe because she saw him through new eyes, Alexander appeared to be growing more thin by the day. When she mentioned it to Alex, he shook his head.

"He's the same as always, hon. Maybe a bit pale, but he doesn't look near as bad as he did when he was at death's door a few months ago."

That was when she'd overheard the conversation between Alexander and his son, which had prompted her leaving. Shutting that out of her mind, she touched the pearls at her throat, Alex's gift to her. Somehow, she felt Sabrina's spirit was present in the church with the rest of her family. Daphne knew Sabrina had to be very proud of her son, and her husband, and her newborn granddaughters.

Alexander looked handsome, leaning on his cane and wearing a black suit. Alex was a younger version of his father, looking very much like the strong, active man they'd watched riding his horse across the pastures on the movie screen the other night.

Danita and Cos looked the way they always did,

gently worn, homespun and happy. Cos had his arm around Danita, and she clung tightly to his other arm.

The babies looked like fairy princesses in their gowns. Every time Daphne thought about the trouble Alexander had gone through to get these most special gifts, tears pressured her eyes. He should have been at home resting. Instead, he'd searched for gifts that would please her heart and showcase the very way she intended to raise her children—unique in their individuality.

She was touched in a way she couldn't have imagined.

They responded to the questions the minister asked and repeated the vows. Danielle Constance and Sabrina Caroline wailed when they left their parents' arms to be held by the minister, but Alexis Abigail only stared patiently at the adult faces looking at her. After the holy water had been placed on her head, her grandfather swiftly handed his cane to Sinclair and rescued her, tucking her safely into his arms. Alexis gave him a smile, her very first. The sun streamed through the stunning stained-glass windows of the church the first Banning family had attended, and Daphne felt blessed. All the old heartaches, all the ill feelings, were washed away.

She closed her eyes and prayed this magical moment would last forever.

It was not to be. In the night, Alexander Banning Senior slipped away, his fingers clutching a picture of his wife and himself on the day they'd brought their baby home to Green Forks.

Alex.

THE LOSS of his father was something Alex had expected. In fact, the birth of his girls had given his father something to live for, making a recovery that had surprised even the physicians. So he was able to lay his father to rest with a true sense of contentment mixed with wistful sadness. No one knew better than he that his father had finally become a happy man before he died. Alex owed that knowledge to Daphne.

Unfortunately, his wife was shattered by Alexander's passing. It was as if something unsaid between the two of them had gone to the grave with Alexander. Daphne returned to her cozy apartment one afternoon, nearly driving Alex mad with worry that she wouldn't return.

When she did, she had a beautiful stained-glass frame she'd fashioned in her studio. The frame had three red and pink hearts, lovely and ephemeral jewel tones in the glass. Each heart held a picture of a baby, as well as a lock of hair and a snip of lace from each baby's christening gown. This frame Daphne quietly slipped into the coffin with Alexander.

His father, Alex knew, would have loved the gift. He tried to comfort Daphne the best he knew how, but she retreated into a shell of formality he couldn't penetrate.

Best for now, he decided, to let her grieve in peace. Daphne was a woman of strong, deep feelings. He appreciated her mourning his father. No doubt hormones still had control over her body, and caring for three babies was a superhuman demand. Everything emotional seemed pinpoint sharp to her. The worst thing, as far as Daphne was concerned, was that Alexander had died three days before Alex's and Daphne's anniversary. His wife paced at night like a wraith who couldn't find peace. He began to grow extremely concerned for her health.

He wondered if the answer was to get her out of the house for a while. Alex took her for a long drive, but she fretted the whole time to get back to her babies. He sighed as his wife retreated into her quarters and decided not to press her further. Tomorrow was a big day. Daphne would have her two-weeks-after-delivery checkup, which he couldn't help but think was a good thing. He intended to mention to the physician how much strain his wife was under.

The other event of the day would be the reading of the will. Alex was ready to get past the solicitor's visit.

Then they would have an elaborate candlelight dinner at home, since Daphne wasn't comfortable leaving the babies for long. This way he could celebrate their anniversary with his wife in a relaxed yet romantic way. He intended to tell her tomorrow night, in case there was any way she could have missed his feelings, how very much he loved her and wanted her to stay with him at Green Forks.

All in all, tomorrow, momentous as it was, promised to be a day of putting things to rest and starting anew.

The doorbell chimed deep and low in the hallway. Alex retreated to the safety of a room, not in the mood for a condolence visit. Neighbors had come from all over town bearing gifts of food and sympathy. He was grateful for their efforts, but right now his mind was too tangled up over Daphne to make social conversation.

"Sinclair, you old bag of bones, you haven't changed much in twenty years, have you?"

Alex cocked his head at the shrill, garrulous tone. His butler murmured something in response.

"Get my bags, and Phillip's, and be quick about it," the authoritative voice commanded.

Visitors? Alex wondered. He didn't know anyone had been invited. Perhaps Alexander had contacted these people before he died and forgotten to mention it to him. Striding out to meet the unexpected guests, he stared at the staggering amount of luggage on the pavement.

Whoever this woman with the towering, unfashionable hat and her tall, soft-looking companion were, they planned on staying a long time.

Chapter Nine

Alex met them on the top step of the porch, his brows lowered. "I'm Alex Banning. I apologize, but you have me at a disadvantage." He looked the woman over. She instantly puffed like a peacock.

Daphne walked to her husband's side, intending to help Alex meet his surprise guests. The woman gave her a disdainful once-over, dismissing her as unimportant. Daphne stiffened at the obvious dislike in her eyes.

"I'm your aunt, Beatrice Banning Carlton," she announced loudly. "This is your cousin, Phillip. And this is his wife, Gloria."

A tall, obviously pregnant brunette, looking a little green, got out of the car. Daphne surmised she hadn't enjoyed the trip from wherever they'd come. So recently pregnant herself, she felt sorry for the woman's plight.

"I don't have an Aunt Beatrice." Alex's voice was stern.

"Oh, yes, you do." Aunt Beatrice gave Alex a poke in the chest with a short digit. "And I'm her."

His gaze swept disdainfully to the offending finger.

It was promptly removed, but Aunt Beatrice's face pinched like she'd swallowed fermented apple cider.

"My father never mentioned you."

"Of course he didn't. He had his reasons."

"I'm sure you are mistaken, madam. There has been only one child born to each Banning family—until now," he said with a glance at Daphne. "This has been the case for several generations."

The tenseness in Alex radiated to Daphne. She put her hand on his upper arm to show her support, feeling his tightly bunched muscle. Obviously this woman was an imposter, an ambulance chaser of the worst kind. She was sorry Alex had to deal with this unpleasantness while his grief was still fresh. His face looked as though it had been carved from stone.

By contrast, Phillip appeared gleeful, while Gloria's gaze roamed every inch of the magnificent mansion. She had completely lost her greenish tinge, the sight of the Banning property seemingly reviving her greatly.

"Even if you were remotely connected to my father in some way," Alex stated harshly, "he passed away a few days ago. You've just missed his funeral."

"Oh, I know all about that," she said airily. "It's rude to keep your aunt standing in the driveway like we're not family, Alex. Move out of the way so Sinclair can see to my bags. We've had a long journey from Philly and we're pooped."

Daphne's jaw dropped as Aunt Beatrice didn't offer even a word of condolence to Alex. Staring at her wrinkled, triumphant face, intuition hit Daphne.

It was an ambush. Alex and Green Forks were under attack.

"What do you know about this?" Alex whispered to Sinclair, who had picked up the suitcases as he had been bid. Alex held Daphne's hand tightly as they walked down the long entry hall. "Is she really my father's sister?"

"I'm afraid so," Sinclair murmured. He met Alex's gaze apologetically.

"Why don't I know about her?" Alex demanded.

"I'm sorry, sir. It's not for me to say." The butler's expression was worried.

"I'll have Nelly show you to your rooms," Alex said over his shoulder to the group staring at the sculptures adorning the entry hall. He pressed an intercom button, which brought Nelly within moments. In a low tone, he said, "Please show our guests to some quarters, Nelly. As far away from my father's, and Daphne's, as possible, please."

"How about the wing that never got renovated, sir?"

"Very good." He stepped back so his unwelcome visitors could pass.

"Be quick with our luggage, Sinclair," Aunt Beatrice said as she swept by. "I will need to change for dinner."

"She acts like this is a palace." Perplexed, Alex watched his newfound aunt make a grand exit. "She's going to be surprised when she learns that this is a working ranch, not Windsor Castle."

Sinclair cleared his throat. "I believe she perceives

herself to be from the upper crust of society, sir. I'd better get these bags up to her."

"Wait." Alex stopped Sinclair. "If my father didn't want me to know about her, obviously they weren't close. Why is she here?"

"Because he's gone," Sinclair said simply.

Daphne felt her husband's hand tighten in hers. "Fine. But why didn't she attend the funeral?"

"Oh, she won't be interested in grieving," Sinclair said softly. "I imagine she's after her, um—" He swallowed his words, looking sorrowed that he'd overstepped his place by starting to offer an unflattering judgment.

Alex stared hard at his butler. "Did you call and tell her Dad had died?"

"No, sir. That would not have been my place."

"Then the family lawyer did."

"I'm sure that was the case." Sinclair's eyelids lowered slowly as he turned to his work. "I hear the beldam calling from her lair," he said under his breath. "I'd best get the dolly for all they've brought."

Sinclair hurried off. Alex stared after him. "I don't understand," he muttered. "Why didn't Dad tell me?"

Daphne curled her fingers into his. "He must have had his reasons."

"Yeah, but it feels all wrong. He had to have known they'd show up on his doorstep wanting whatever they thought they could get." Alex stared at her, his eyes puzzled. "I can't think of one single reason my father wouldn't tell me about a sister, especially if he did leave her something. He had to have known how extraordinarily uncomfortable it would be to have her show up without warning.''

Daphne ran her fingertips along his brow, trying to smooth his frown. ''I'm sure he acted for the best,'' she soothed. ''I never knew your father to act without reason. He was hot-tempered, but he was also a strategist. He spent a lot of hours up in his room plotting.''

Alex smiled. ''Are you saying he was a manipulative old man?''

''No.'' She shook her head. ''I'm saying that he loved you with his whole heart. If he didn't tell you there was an Aunt Beatrice, he must have had a darn good reason.''

ALEX WAS on the phone with the family lawyer when Daphne found her way to Alexander's old quarters after checking on the babies. Alex had legal documents laid out in front of him on the desk where his father had once sat.

''So you did call them, then.''

Daphne winced at her husband's authoritative tone.

''And she is truly my father's sister?''

He ran a hand down the back of his neck, nodding at Daphne as she hovered in the doorway. He pointed to the old rocking chair. Daphne sat, somehow glad Alex didn't mind her listening in on his conversation.

She'd like to be with him if he needed her.

''You could have at least let me know there was such a relative,'' Alex stated. ''If Sinclair hadn't vouched for her, I would have directed the whole family to hit the road.''

He listened for a moment. Daphne hovered on the seat edge.

"Well, can you at least tell me what they think they're getting of my father's? The way they're acting—and by the amount of luggage they've got—they seem to think they're staying a while."

After a suspended moment, he said, "Fine. Get yourself over here by two o'clock today." He hung up and stood to push the intercom.

"Yes?" Sinclair's voice asked.

"Will you tell our guests that the family solicitor will arrive at two o'clock to discuss my father's will?"

"Yes, sir."

Alex took his finger off the intercom and leaned forward, palms on the desk. Daphne watched him anxiously.

"I have a real bad feeling about this."

"I'm starting to get one myself," she said, trying to sound light. Her heart went out to him. How badly he must feel! Yet she didn't dare put her arms around him and hold him the way she wanted to. Tomorrow was their anniversary, and the time she'd agreed to stay in this house would be over. "I'm so sorry about everything," she murmured. "What a nasty shock."

"Yeah." He swiveled to face her and leaned against the desk in a pose that was anything but relaxed. His anguished eyes spoke of the pain he suffered. "Why didn't he tell me, Daph?"

Their eyes locked. "I don't know," she whispered uncertainly. Silent communication passed between them, but it was garbled and unreadable. She didn't know what to say to him.

"I keep asking myself why. Why? I thought we were close. I mean, we weren't for a long time. I had my rebellious stage like most other teenagers. But we worked it out. Some people never do, you know?" His mouth flattened in an unhappy line. "But my dad, Daph, my dad was my...best friend." The first tears she'd seen him shed since his father died brightened his eyes. "I never needed a best friend because I had him. Then I met you, and for the first time in my life, I had two."

She couldn't help herself. She flew out of the chair and threw her arms around his neck. "Oh, Alex! I am so sorry! So very sorry!"

He put his head in the crook of her neck, his forehead resting on her shoulder, and shuddered with heartbreak. Daphne blinked back tears of her own, holding on to him for all she was worth. "How can I help you, Alex?" she whispered. "How can I make you feel better?"

"Just be with me," he murmured after a moment. He took a fortifying breath of air. "I need you, Daph."

She held him tighter but made no reply. Now wasn't the time to hold back from him. Right now he had to deal with Aunt Beatrice, Phillip and Gloria, and learn what secret Alexander Banning had been hiding.

In the meantime, she meant to have a talk with Alexander. It was past time.

LEAVING ALEX to look over his father's papers, Daphne walked from the room. How could they have known Alexander would die so suddenly? There was so much she'd wanted to talk to him about. She had wanted to know, in her heart, that whatever had been worrying him the day she'd overheard his conversation with Alex was water under the bridge. It seemed imperative that she explain there would be no more children. By his heartfelt gift of christening gowns to the babies, Daphne knew he loved them.

But he'd expected more.

She felt like an imposter, a fake.

Walking in front of the portraits in the long, winding hall, she stopped in front of Alexander's. "I want to talk to you."

His grim, aristocratic eyebrows furrowed at her. Eyes of blue stone stared into her soul. A slit of a mouth gave the impression that he had disdained the artist's attempt to capture his spirit on canvas. Wild black hair was tousled, as if he'd just come in off a horse. It was the image of a younger Alexander, a stubborn, determined rock in the landscape of Green Forks Ranch.

"I love your son," she told the portrait. "No matter how much I wish I could give him what you thought you were getting when you bought those rangy cows from my father, you ended up getting the short end of the stick." She took a deep breath as he stared at her. "I suppose I should laugh myself silly that, after your disgraceful conduct at the dinner table the other night when you accused my father of swindling you, you can now actually consider yourself cheated.''

Daphne ignored the chills running up and down her arms and continued. ''I know you can hear me. So I'm going to tell you now what I should have told you before.'' She drew a deep, shaking breath. ''I can't have any more children. Those three little granddaughters are all I have to give this family.''

He watched her relentlessly.

''There won't be a boy, Alexander. So your well-thought-out plan didn't work. Oh, I know what you thought you were buying. My mom had six sons, and you thought my genes might bear you just one. But what you don't know is that I didn't marry your son because he was a Banning or because of his money. I was probably more content being poor and on my own in my little apartment than I am now. So that's where we stand. I love your son. But I didn't produce the heir I was expected to, and I don't know if I can stay with Alex because of it.''

The eyes didn't blink. If anything, they seemed to glow, as if any second the portrait might speak. ''One more thing, Alexander. I'm not sure I ever told you I loved you when you were alive. I think I've been too afraid to tell you. You were pompous and arrogant and a stubborn old donkey, but I loved you, Alexander Banning, and I'm sorry I didn't say so when you were alive. No doubt I would have gotten an impatient *hmph!* for my efforts, but at least it would have been said.''

She waited, her arms crossed rebelliously. ''What's the matter? No retort?'' She shook her head. ''It doesn't feel right, Alexander, me getting the last word. I have a funny feeling nothing's ever going to feel right again, without your bellow rattling the roof. Did you know that every time you stomped up the stairs, Sinclair and Nelly had to straighten the portraits?''

His eyes held a cagey gleam. ''Of course you did. That's why you did it, you ornery old thing. You liked knowing people were taking care of you. You liked knowing you could affect their lives.'' She ran a wistful hand over the frame of his picture. ''Well, your sister is here, and something tells me if you were still around, Sinclair and Nelly would be doing a hell of a lot of picture straightening today.''

She backed away from the portrait. Her eyes held the painted ones, mesmerized. The strangest sense of doom suddenly assailed her, and she could no longer look Alexander in the eye.

Chapter Ten

The reading of the will commenced at two o'clock that afternoon. Daphne was seated next to Alex. Beatrice, Phillip and Gloria hovered on the edges of brocaded chairs, their expressions like expectant hawks, not even a mild attempt to appear regretful that Alexander was gone. It made Daphne sick to her stomach. *I'd give anything to have that complaining old man back, and they're just glad he's gone,* she thought angrily.

Nelly and Sinclair were also seated in the library, in chairs off to the side. To her surprise, Cos and Danita came in at the last moment. The youthful solicitor nodded from his place behind a wide mahogany desk before leaning to adjust the curtain panels to block the sunlight that streamed onto the papers in front of him.

"Now that we're all here," he said nervously, "I will introduce myself. I am Joshua Farling, a representative of the law firm from which Alexander Banning required services." He nodded toward Beatrice's contingent. "I want to express my sincere sorrow to all of you at the loss of a man you all loved."

"Where's the old guy my brother had under his thumb?" Beatrice demanded suspiciously.

"As I mentioned to Alex on the phone," the lawyer replied, running a hand over the knot in his tie, "his father's previous lawyer had to leave the country unexpectedly on urgent business."

"Likely story." Beatrice waved an imperious hand. "Get on with it, then."

Daphne felt frozen and out of place, but she touched her hand to her husband's. He squeezed her fingers lightly and raised his eyebrows in a wish-this-was-over expression.

She wished it was over, too, and that they could leave the anticipatory Beatrice behind.

"Alexander provided in his will monetary amounts for his two loyal retainers, Nelly and Sinclair." Joshua named sums that seemed staggering to Daphne. "It was his wish that the two of you live on these grounds for as long as you desire employment at Green Forks."

For some reason, Joshua sent a stern look toward Beatrice. Daphne prayed her sudden stomachache would go away. She had the baby monitor with her so she could hear the babies if any of them awakened from their nap, but they were silent. She desperately wanted to leave the stiff, almost predatory atmosphere in this room. If Alex hadn't needed her support, she would have made her excuses. For his sake, she remained still.

"For Cos and Danita Way, I have a letter." Joshua handed across a thin white envelope.

Cos wouldn't take it, so Danita did. "Dear Cos and

Danita,'' she read aloud. "As it was no secret to anyone that you would outlive me, I have written this letter concerning the recent purchase I made from your ranch. My relationship with your family has always been a difficult one. I didn't much like you, Cos, for many years, and that's something you won't be surprised to hear. Many times I thought about sending my legal representative to simply offer you more money than you'd ever dreamed of for your ranch so I wouldn't have to look at you anymore. However, even I am not that much of a coward. Your small, piddly spread of land seemed to hold all of that which I did not have, and I was jealous.

"Yes, I bought those cows knowing they were more valuable than you were aware. And I was glad when Alex brought Daphne to my home, because she was your only daughter. Far as I could see, I had you over a barrel, Cos, at last.

"But since you've outlived me, my triumph is short-lived. My solicitor will be returning to you the deed of sale for the cattle. The money I paid you need not be returned, for obvious reasons, my being dead the first of them. This is a bequest I am leaving to you and Danita because I don't want it on my conscience when I go to my grave. The better man has won, Cos, but I can rest easy knowing the children your daughter will bear Alex will wear your brand of honesty. Sincerely, Alexander Banning.''

Danita looked up from the letter, her eyes meeting Daphne's. "That's all it says.''

Daphne held back a groan. She couldn't meet Alex's eyes. His father was making her feel guilty even from the grave! There would be no sons, no more children. Alexander had gambled on her and lost. *It's your own fault for meddling,* she told Alexander mentally. *You got your power and privilege confused with people's lives.*

"And that brings us to the matter of Green Forks," Joshua said after handing Danita a tissue. He sent Alex a worried stare. "According to this document, which is British in origin, Alex, you are entitled to all funds and money from your father's estate as his only heir. However, the house, any lands that were bought before your father's possession of the ranch, and the contents of the estate that were part of the family inheritance are subject to the entailment provision originally set up by the founding members who bought the Green Forks property."

"What the hell does that mean?" Alex rose from his chair.

"It means that, for the past several generations, Green Forks itself has been in the possession of male children of the first Banning, Alexander the First. And so, in turn, it will entail to your male child or children. If there are none, the property will pass to Beatrice's son, and then his son."

"What?" Alex demanded. "This is my home! An American court of law will find that to be the case. I don't care where the original owners of the estate were from or where they're buried." He paced the room, stiff with rage and astonishment. "I've lived here, worked this land! How could it belong to people I never even knew about?"

"I'm not quite certain of this myself," Joshua admitted. "I'm new to the firm, but I'll need to look into this matter further. However, as it stands, Beatrice and her family must be considered in the event you have no male heir."

"This is preposterous!" Alex glanced around the room, reminding Daphne of Alexander Senior. Impatient, wanting to hear answers that would favor his temper.

Cold fear swept over Daphne as the true enormity of Alexander's gamble struck.

Gloria smiled and laid a manicured hand over her distended middle. "I'm having a boy."

"OF ALL THE ridiculous things!" Alex paced in Daphne's quarters, wild-eyed after the lawyer had left. "Why didn't my father tell me?" He whirled to stare at her.

She cradled a fussy baby in her arms and shook her head. "Maybe he didn't want to put any pressure on you, Alex. It certainly seems your father was carrying around enough of it for the both of you."

"Yeah, but…damn it!" He sank into a chair. "How could he not mention that the roof over my head and the ranch I spent my sweat and blood investing in wasn't even mine?"

Daphne put Danielle to her breast. Alex watched, momentarily distracted.

"I don't know," Daphne replied, "except that he didn't know for sure you weren't going to have a son. He couldn't predict that, Alex. Green Forks *is* yours, until…later."

"So I work my butt off to turn the whole thing

over to Phillip?'' His incredulous tone threw an emotional knife into her, which she knew he didn't intend.

"He tried his best to preserve the line by getting you married to me,'' she said miserably.

"What the hell does that mean?''

"You know exactly!'' she cried. "Let's not pretend anymore! Your father needed sons to keep this ranch in your hands. My mother had borne six of them.'' Her baby stopped nursing, its attention caught by Daphne's tone. For some reason, anger at the situation suddenly flared inside her. "Alex, I overheard your father talking to you. He said he'd arranged our marriage. It's clear your father thought he was buying those stupid cows as an installment payment, which is just as chauvinistic as that entailment provision on Green Forks. But the fact is, he thought he was getting a sure bet at male heirs to secure this place for you.''

"Chauvinistic? You think the entailment provision is chauvinistic?''

She paused, hearing something in his tone she couldn't label. "Well, yes. Of course I do. I mean, how old-fashioned can you get? Women can do things as well as men. They're certainly no less capable. It's the way I intend to approach rearing my daughters. Would you have me teach them that they are second best to men?''

"Hell, no!''

"Well, you wouldn't be in this snarl if the Banning men hadn't had a rather narrow view of women. Obviously, Beatrice feels she's entitled to something, and we don't know that she isn't right.'' She took a deep breath, anguished. "All I know is, I can't stay married to you knowing I've cost you what you love the most."

Alex's jaw sagged. "Daphne, you've gotten something confused, or a lot of things confused, but you're wrong on just about everything you just said. Dad liked to think he was a king who arranged things at the crook of a finger but he didn't arrange our marriage. And I sure as hell wouldn't have married anybody I didn't love even if I had known about the entailment. Which I didn't, so that should ease your mind. Leave my father's maneuvering out of this, hon." He crossed the room to put his arms around her. "There has to be something we can do."

"Not without me being able to conceive again." She couldn't meet his gaze.

"This is crazy! I can't believe my whole way of life revolves around whether I got my wife pregnant with the right kind of baby." He lowered himself to the edge of the bed, taking Daphne with him in his lap. "Okay," he said with a long sigh. "So what? We still have each other. We'll just have to live here with Phillip and Gloria and Beatrice. It'll be like a 'Dallas' rerun, but I suppose there's no way around it."

Her heart beat crazily. "Alex, I'm not living here with them." She would never be able to look at Gloria's growing stomach knowing that child was the one who would inherit what Alex should have had. "I am going ahead with the divorce."

"The hell you are." He pushed her against the sheets gently and took his time kissing her neck.

"You can have all the baby blues and pregnancy hormones you want and feel guilty all you like, but you are my wife and you're staying that way, lady."

He ran a hand under her dress.

Daphne heated up like a hot summer day. Reminding herself of their situation, she tried to push his hand—and him—away.

"I can't live here with them," she said desperately. "I *would* feel guilty, Alex. I'm not cut out for living like Sue Ellen Ewing. I'm just a girl from a dirt-poor farm down the road. Intrigue isn't my specialty."

"Mmm," he murmured against her ear, "I like it when you talk like that. Say it again."

"Say what?" One hand caressed her breast, and Daphne's urge to push him away was quickly waning. "Alex…"

"Say that intrigue isn't your specialty."

"Why?" she demanded.

"I like knowing I married an honest woman. That's what my dad was really after, Daph. He said so in the letter he wrote to your father."

"Alex, honesty isn't going to keep this house for you!"

"No," he said, stroking her in places she had forgotten she loved to be stroked by this man, "but you're mine, Daphne Way Banning. I may not be able to keep this ranch forever, but I can keep you. And I'm going to."

He lowered his mouth to her lips and stroked the most sensitive part of her body over and over again. Daphne gasped as spasms washed over her. He cradled her in his arms, holding her tightly the way she'd always liked to be held when they'd made love.

But he couldn't hold her forever, because she wasn't a possession, which ran counter to the Banning male thought process. He might not give her a divorce, but she wasn't staying in a house where she didn't belong to watch another woman give birth to what she hadn't been able to.

For the first time, Daphne truly understood why Alexander Senior had felt the way he had. She tasted the bitter envy he had drunk for many of his days.

And she knew that, just as it had poisoned his life, the envy would poison her life with Alex.

ALEX SLIPPED AWAY from Daphne's side as she lay sleeping. He checked on the babies, none of whom appeared to be ready to awaken. Danita said they were in a resting period of their lives, recovering from being pushed out into the world.

He understood that feeling. The afternoon with the lawyer had pushed him out into the world, and if he could have, he, too, would be sleeping.

There wasn't time for that. He needed to talk to Beatrice and see exactly what she planned to do. Surely that particularly ugly arm of his family didn't plan on staying? Maybe they meant to get what they could and run. People who had never worked land usually didn't have an appreciation for it. They only saw the money the soil could yield. Perhaps a check or two every year would see them on their way to Philly.

In the great hall, he found Sinclair and Nelly working quietly. One by one, they had removed the ancestral portraits from the walls. Dark outlines on the silk-papered walls gave a naked and harsh appearance to the staircase.

"What are you doing?" he demanded.

Nelly and Sinclair jumped in tandem, the picture of his father bumping oddly between them.

"Oh, sir, Ms. Beatrice told us to take down all these portraits." Nelly's red, twisted hair was completely askew with her efforts. Tiny beads of sweat dotted her face, but it was her eyes that held the most distress. "She said a female's running the ranch now, and we don't need to be looking at a bunch of dead men in out-of-date suits."

Sinclair met Alex's eyes, chagrined. "We're wrapping them carefully for storage. Ms. Beatrice says we're to have the walls repapered in gold and have a decorator in to choose more modern artwork. Copies, of course, but something suitable to her taste."

"I see." Fury boiled inside Alex. Did Beatrice think she could just come into his home and rip apart the very fabric that seamed the memories and heritage of Green Forks? A female running the ranch, indeed. He'd never thought of himself as a true chauvinist, but he felt that Beatrice was more likely to ruin the ranch than run it. "I will have to speak to my long-lost aunt."

"She's in the parlor, sir." Sinclair looked away, while Nelly looked at the patterned carpet beneath her feet.

It wasn't their fault, and Alex didn't want them

feeling he was angry with them. Without another word, he strode to the parlor.

Gloria and Phillip were ensconced in chairs on opposite sides of the room, apparently having a long-distance conversation. Beatrice eyed some papers she held in her hands.

She glanced up and motioned to him. "Come on in," she stated with an imperative wave of her hand. "I want to talk to you about these." The papers she held fluttered as she thrust them at him. "What, exactly, is Green Forks worth? I can't tell from this statement."

His jaw dropped as he glanced at his father's private bank statement. "Where did you get this?"

"From Alexander's office," she said, thrusting her chin at him belligerently.

He gave her a narrow stare. "You did not inherit my father's personal money and acquisitions."

"No, but I want to make sure I'm being treated fairly." She thrust a finger toward the papers. "So tell me what I'm worth. I don't want to call that lawyer back to the house. No doubt he charges a bundle for his services. I'll have to hire a solicitor immediately who can sift through all these documents, just in case your father's lawyer might be of a mind to play partial."

"I don't appreciate your insinuation." Alex stared at her, his posture stiff. "But you don't inherit a dime until after I'm gone, as I see it. You're far overstepping your due place."

"Don't give me that." She snapped her fingers at

him as if he were an inattentive dog. "It's time for better treatment of my side of the family."

He shook his head. "Why would you be treated unfairly?"

Her eyes turned to angry slits. "As long as Alexander was alive, he could pretend I didn't exist. Well, I do, and I'm here now, and I'm going to be accorded respect."

Alex frowned. "What exactly was the reason for your estrangement from my father?" He felt like he was dealing with a dark wall of mystery. Until he knew what was behind the wall, he couldn't knock it down.

"The reason—" Beatrice bit the words off "—was that our parents died in a car accident. Rather than take care of me as a brother should, Alexander sent me off to live with our mother's relatives. I was just ten," she said defensively. "He was eighteen, and even then determined to have Green Forks only for himself. I was too young to know how I was being shuffled off, never to know that my birthright was at risk."

"That doesn't sound like my father." What harm could his sister do his father? The entailment favored male children. Beatrice wouldn't have been a threat.

"Don't kid yourself. The men in this family come from a long line of thieves and cheats. Your father was one of the better ones."

Alex shifted uncomfortably. Hadn't his father admitted cheating Cos with great enthusiasm the night they'd eaten together? And he'd said as much in his letter. "My understanding is that men of integrity have built this ranch,'' he said stiffly. "A few CEOs, a wildcatter—''

"Oh, spare me.'' Gloria giggled as Beatrice snorted. Phillip wore an amused grin. "Not one of them would have ever made it into a social register of worth. Money was the only thing that separated any of those men from the title of petty bank robber. No princes in this family, I can assure you.'' She smiled benignly at her son. "But Phillip has been raised to know the meaning of honesty. Integrity. And he will bring credit to the family name when it's his turn.''

Alex bit the inside of his jaw. "Can we get back to the situation between my father and you?''

"Your father,'' Beatrice said acidly, "being a cheat and a thief, paid our mother's side of the family handsomely to keep me away. I waited, day after lonely day, for some word from my brother, whom I loved dearly. But he never wrote, never called. Sent a check every year, a bribe to keep me up north.'' She sighed dramatically. "I had no idea the insignificant funds he sent barely touched the wealth he was enjoying.'' Her expression was long-suffering.

"And how did you discover that my father was...cheating you?''

"When I became of legal age, the meager checks he sent were turned over to me. That's when I first knew something was very wrong. Why did my dear brother not invite me to live in Texas with him?'' she asked, her mouth pinched with pity. "I wrote him, but he only sent another check in reply, a raise in funds, if you will. By then I had met a man I loved, and I married him, staying among friends and family as my brother clearly saw no need to reconcile himself with me.''

''I see.'' Alex moved toward the bar, pouring himself a straight whiskey. Was it true? Could his father really have paid his sister off in this manner? He'd paid Cos off to get his daughter, if Daphne's theory was to be believed.

''It was clear he didn't want me around,'' she said sadly, ''and when my husband died, I thought he might invite his poor sister to live with him then, but no. There I was up north, with no idea that my brother was living like a king.''

Out of the corner of his eye, he saw Daphne stroll the babies into the room.

''What are those?'' Beatrice demanded.

''Our children.'' He smiled reassuringly at Daphne. Her face was pale and drawn.

''I'm going out for a drive,'' she told him.

''If you'll wait five minutes, I'll go with you.''

''I'll be all right.'' Her gaze swept Gloria, then returned like a boomerang to him. ''Goodbye, Alex.'' She turned the stroller, the three little heads with three little white bonnets inside glancing around with interest.

Alex felt a momentary pang as he stared at his daughters. They looked like angels! He wished he could give them the security of Green Forks, but he couldn't. Instantly, Alex knew that same feeling had driven his father. Not that Alexander's manipulative ways could ever be excused, but for the first time, he recognized the burning need to provide for and protect his children. Daphne's posterior swayed enticingly as she pushed the stroller through the wide doorway, her bronze hair falling in feminine curls down her back.

Oh, he definitely understood the urge to provide for and protect.

"You must be disappointed that all those children are girls."

"Not a bit," Alex assured her, raw dislike tearing into him. Until now, he'd been too numbed by Beatrice's arrival to feel one way or the other toward her. But now he sampled his father's dislike for her. "My family is my pride and joy."

"Well." She settled into the chair. "I hope so. Because as far as I can see, they're all you've got."

"I fail to see your point."

"Well, let me make it clear, then." She shot him a smile that was meant to needle. "We're going to live here, Phillip, Gloria and I. We're putting down permanent roots at Green Forks. As Gloria is having a son, that puts us in charge for the future. As you so succinctly put it, the entailment won't hold water over here in America. You can play it that way if you like so that you'll have the upper hand during your lifetime. It won't matter, because I'm suing for the portion that by rights is mine. Alexander and I should have inherited equally upon our parents' deaths. I may be a woman, but I'm not stupid," she said with a jaundiced smile, "and as far as I can see, I'm due a hell of a lot of back interest on what was stolen from me. Either way you move, you're going to lose."

"That sounds like a threat." He pinned her with a relentless stare.

She returned it, her smile never faltering. "It is, my dear nephew. Because if I learned anything during my exile, it is that blood is thinner than the almighty dollar bill." She shrugged. "You of all people can't expect me to feel any differently, as you are the son of the greatest cheat and thief the Banning lineage ever begot."

Chapter Eleven

"From here on, we'll let our lawyers hammer this out." There wasn't much else Alex could say to Beatrice's pronouncement, though he hated to declare war on his own flesh and blood. She was determined to protect her place and Phillip's—and his unborn son's—with the same fierceness that had possessed Alexander Senior.

Nodding briskly at Beatrice, who smiled with great enjoyment at his discomfort, Alex left the large room and headed to Daphne's quarters. He needed his wife and his children.

"They've gone, sir," Nelly told him dolefully. "Miss Daphne said to tell you that she stayed as long as she'd agreed to. And in light of the situation, she thought it would be easier on you if she went on her way."

Alex's mind went blank with astonishment. Daphne had deserted him? His heart constricted tightly and painfully as his disbelieving gaze roamed the room, looking for any sign that Daphne might not have yet left. The three white-painted cribs were being dismantled, and a stray box of diaper wipes sat on the bureau, but that was all. For the second time, she'd left him—and he was furious.

"Why are you taking those down?" he demanded. "Daphne will need those cribs when I drag her back here."

Sinclair shook his head. "She asked that they be sent over to her. Everything else she had loaded into the Suburban."

"Damn it!" He ground his teeth. "Did she say where she was going?"

"Not directly, sir." Nelly didn't meet his eyes.

"Okay," he said carefully, recognizing that his faithful servants might be in on a plan with his wife, "can you tell me where these cribs are going?"

"No, sir." Sinclair looked miserable.

"I will find her, you know. Why are you covering her whereabouts?" He bit the inside of his jaw to keep from sternly reminding them whose faithful retainers they were supposed to be.

"She asked us not to say." Nelly folded a baby blanket and met his eyes unhappily. "We know you will find her, so we just don't want to be a party to it."

"You make me sound like I'm going to hunt her down and shoot her."

"No, sir. It's just that she needs some time alone. It's crazy around here, and we understand how she feels." Nelly glanced at Sinclair, who nodded.

"Don't tell me you two are packing up, as well?" Alex didn't know what he would do without them.

"Oh, no, sir. Your father would have wanted us to stay with you. We've been with you since you came screaming into your daddy's life.'' Nelly shook her head. ''But Miss Daphne asked us not to say where she was headed, and we want to keep ourselves out of her business. That's all it is.''

''Fine,'' he snapped. ''I'll find her.''

Sinclair straightened from adjusting a crib. ''Alex,'' he said softly.

''Yes?'' He turned to meet his butler's gaze, his expression hard.

''You had me bring Daphne here as soon as she came home from the hospital.''

He didn't like the almost pleading tone of Sinclair's voice. ''So?''

''And she agreed to stay until your anniversary, which, coincidentally, happens to be today.'' Sinclair pursed his lips. ''She has kept her part of the bargain. May I suggest that to coerce a woman a second time might bring a bad result?''

Alex's brows soared. ''She is my wife.''

''That,'' Sinclair agreed, nodding, ''but not a possession.''

He couldn't believe what he was hearing. ''We have three children! Our place is together!''

''If that's what both parties want, yes. But you've got a bit of your father in you, Alex, which, while usually a good thing, isn't going to help you with Miss Daphne. You cannot force her to be somewhere she doesn't want to be, just because you think it should be so.''

Pain he couldn't identify as logical twisted his gut. He loved Daphne. She couldn't leave him. She loved him. ''I'm not trying to…'' he said in his own defense, then halted. The thought that she would choose to leave him hurt as it had when she'd left him the first time. How in the hell could he be back at square one when they'd had two good weeks together? When they had three perfect daughters to raise?

Reality forced him to admit that they hadn't really had two good weeks. Alexander had died, and the close, together feeling Alex and Daphne had begun to regain had swiftly eroded.

It suddenly occurred to him that Beatrice's snide dig that his father had been the greatest liar and cheat of all, and now Sinclair's assertion that he was like his father—pigheaded—combined to make an unpleasant person. Surely he had treated Daphne with respect? Could it be that he was used to getting his way by whatever means, as his father had done?

As always when faced with a difficult dilemma, he forced himself to defer to Sinclair's wisdom. "What are you suggesting?"

His butler nodded, lowering his eyes. "Perhaps some time apart, sir."

"We've had months apart!"

"Yes. But Miss Daphne is grieving terribly, and struggling with the joys and challenges of three infants." Sinclair kept his gaze fastened to the floor, as did Nelly. "Forgive me for saying so, but this time I can't recommend jewels to soothe the situation." He drew a deep breath that sounded tight and distressed. "This time, sir, you are going to have to wait for Miss Daphne to return to you—on her own."

"I'M HOME, Momma," Daphne called.

She walked into the faded kitchen that lacked fresh

paint but never love and warmth.

At the sink, Danita turned to face her. "You got the babies?"

"I do. Dad's settling them in the spare bedroom." Daphne hovered uncertainly in the doorway. "I hope you don't mind—"

"I don't." Danita came to give her a warm hug. "You're my daughter. Don't say nothing else to me. If you need to be here, that's good enough for me."

"Oh, Momma." Tears stung Daphne's eyes. "I know I should go to my apartment, but I don't want to. I want to be here—"

"Sh." Danita gave her a no-nonsense yet gentle shake. "We've got plenty enough room and some left over. Three little babies oughta be with their grandparents, anyway, not being shuffled around in apartments like a tiny deck of cards." She gave Daphne a thorough eyeing before hugging her again. "You gotta quit wearing yourself so thin, gal. I plan to work on you about this."

Daphne sniffled and laughed in spite of herself. "I think that's why I came home, so you could work on me."

"That's why you've always been smarter than the rest of the pack, Daphne Way. Sooner or later, you let your innate smarts tell ya what to do. Some people want to let their brain tell their hearts what's right, and it don't always work that way. Sometimes, but not always. Sit down, gal. I'll fix you some lunch."

"Thanks, Mom." Daphne sank gratefully into a chair, her frayed nerves beginning to piece together again slowly. It was good to be home, good to be where she knew what to expect. At the Banning mansion, life had been awry moment after moment, always building to a greater crescendo.

She needed calmness right now. Alex did not make her feel calm. He tapped into her wildest emotions, lust, love, anger, denial, delirious happiness. She felt like an old washcloth with the threads worn out.

"What did you tell Alex?"

Daphne closed her eyes. "I didn't."

"You just left?" Danita's eyebrow lifted as she fixed a tuna sandwich.

"I said goodbye, but he was talking to Beatrice and her gang. It didn't look like the conversation was one I should tear him away from, so I left a message with Sinclair and Nelly." She took a grateful drink of the tea Danita put in front of her. "I'll explain everything to him later."

"All right." Danita shrugged, accepting her reasons. "Eat now. You'll need all your strength to face Alex when he comes looking for you."

ALEX DIDN'T COME that entire day. First Daphne was glad, then she was saddened by the fact that it was their anniversary and felt more like a funeral. But she couldn't think about funerals without thinking about Alexander, so after Danita drove her to her two-week checkup and she was pronounced fine, Daphne went home to her babies.

That afternoon the phone rang in her mother's kitchen, but it wasn't Alex. It wasn't even his solicitor, whom she was prepared to hear from because of the children. The afternoon grew longer, and she prayed to get through this one and on to the next. That it was their anniversary made her think about Alex constantly, which wasn't good for the happy mood she was determined to develop.

Tomorrow, she decided, she would clean out her studio and pack up her apartment. She was just wasting money on a place she wasn't going to use anymore. Its purpose was over, and Alex had found her there, anyway.

She was only a stone's throw away, across the road, and he hadn't come to her. Daphne couldn't help feeling a bit irrationally disappointed by that. Not hopeful that he would come, she assured herself, just disappointed. No doubt a normal feeling when a relationship hadn't worked out.

Nightfall came and went. Cicadas sang in the late night breeze, reminding her that autumn always followed summer. She wasn't ready for fall and the ensuing chill of winter, when she had yet to recapture the sunshine in her life.

Depressed, she went to bed after giving the babies a last feeding. They settled in comfortably, their needs for survival met.

Daphne couldn't help wondering if she would ever feel that kind of innocent contentment again.

"DAMN IT!" Alex cursed under his breath as the ladder banged against his shin. Cos's rickety ladder probably wasn't going to hold him up for more than five minutes, but that was all the time he needed to see Daphne. By darn, he was going to see his wife

on their anniversary, even if it meant resorting to unusual methods.

Okay, so maybe his old man's fire burned brightly
within him. But he could temper that, damn it. He
wouldn't drag Daphne from her bedroom and down
the ladder to take her home, even if it was where she
belonged.

The bottom rung cracked when he put a foot on it,
causing a sound loud enough to make the night noises
around him cease. One more loud noise like that, and
old Cos was going to run onto the porch with his
shotgun.

It was worth the risk, he told himself, ascending
the ladder. He knew full well which bedroom was
Daphne's, having thrown rocks against her window
during their courtship. Cradling a full bouquet of
long-stemmed red roses against his chest, Alex prayed
the ladder would hold.

It did, and he gained the top rung, peering in the
darkened window through the small space between
the lace draperies. He couldn't see anything, but in
case she had the babies in there with her, he would
tap softly. Just loud enough to wake his wife.

He raised his hand to tap the glass. The draperies
were shoved back, the window flew up, and Cos's
shotgun poked out.

"Aah!" Alex cried. The ladder swayed precari-
ously, and he dropped the roses as he grabbed the
windowsill.

"Who the hell's out there?" Cos demanded.
"Speak up! My wife's calling the law, but like as not
I'll shoot ya fulla holes 'fore they get here!"

"It's Alex!" To die by Cos's shotgun after the years of feuding were over was too much. He reached out and carefully turned the shotgun aside. Cos's angry face poked out the window, meeting him nose to nose.

"What the hell you doing coming in my window, boy?"

Alex's heartbeat thundered like wild horses. The sight of Cos, his hair standing on end from sleep, was almost more disconcerting than the shotgun he'd been pointing. "I have to see Daphne."

"What'sa matter? Those hooty-snoots kick you out?" Cos glared at him. Danita peered over his shoulder at Alex, her head wrapped in some pink foam thing. "Lookee here, Danita. Now I've got me a Banning trying to creep in my winder to steal my daughter. Again."

Alex didn't bother to dignify that with an answer. "Can I see her, please?"

"There a reason you can't use the phone and ask her?" Cos's chin thrust belligerently out.

Alex leaned back—not enough to tip himself off the ladder. "I didn't think she'd take my call."

"And you'd be thinking right! So how come you're trying to sneak into my house if you know she doesn't want to see ya right now?"

It was a precarious thing, being elevated on a stolen ladder trying to explain to his father-in-law that he only wanted to see Daphne and give her some flowers. Alex sighed, realizing he'd have been better off having the florist deliver some.

"Oh, Cos, for heaven's sake," Danita said, pushing

her husband out of the way. "You act like Alex is doing something you've never done."

"Woman!" Cos roared, apparently not liking this aspect of his matrimonial laundry being aired.

"Go away," she instructed him. "Alex, you've got the wrong bedroom."

"This used to be hers," he said, honestly confused.

"We switched because she needed more room. She's downstairs in the back bedroom. I'm not authorizing you to upset her," she said sternly. "Daphne needs some time to gather herself up. But if you're on a romantic mission to deliver those flowers and nothing else, then you have my permission to do so."

"Thank you, Danita." He glanced cautiously over her shoulder at her husband, who obviously didn't like those arrangements one bit.

"Put the ladder back against the tree," she instructed.

"Yes, ma'am."

"And don't stay long."

"I won't," he agreed.

"She needs her sleep."

"I agree," he said hastily. He descended the ladder and snatched up the roses, which were slightly crumpled from the whole affair.

"And Alex?"

"Yes?"

"Happy anniversary." The window shut with a squeal and a thump.

Alex carried the ladder to its former place, shaking his head. This was not the way he had envisioned spending his anniversary. He was lucky not to have been shot.

For that matter, he was lucky not to be signing divorce papers. He strode around to the side of the house Danita had mentioned and rapped softly on the window.

A second later, a light went on inside. Daphne appeared in the window like a graceful vision. She didn't wear one of the pink foam things her mother had on—nor Cos's angry frown. The window slid up. Alex's blood raced as Daphne met his gaze. A thousand emotions passed between them, none slow enough that he could identify them.

All he knew was that Daphne took his breath away.

"Happy anniversary," he said huskily.

"Same to you." Her large green eyes held astonishment—and did he dare hope happiness?—at his arrival. He handed her the bouquet of red roses.

"Thank you," she said, taking them carefully. "You had yellow roses put in my bedroom at your house. You're spending an awful lot on flowers."

"You're worth it. And this time I wanted red. It's supposed to express a certain emotion." He told her with his eyes what that emotion was.

"I like red." She put the roses on a table in her room and returned to the window. "How did you know I was here?"

"I—uh, your mother told me."

"She did? I thought she was in bed."

He winced. "Where are my daughters?"

Daphne pointed to the room across the hall. "Sleeping comfortably in one of my brothers' old rooms.'' She hesitated, her eyes locking with his. ''You're welcome to visit the babies anytime you like.''

''I know that.'' He was silent for a moment. ''Daphne, you should have told me you were leaving.''

''I couldn't. I mean, I think I would have, but you were busy at the time.'' Uncomfortable, she took a deep breath. ''I was glad, to tell the truth. I knew you'd try to stop me, and I was determined to go.''

That hurt much more than falling off the ladder would have. Alex rubbed at a splinter he'd caught in his palm, a minor annoyance when real pain was in his heart. ''Do you just need time?''

''I don't know.'' She rubbed her arms, shrugging. ''I need to…sort things out.''

''How much time?'' He didn't think he could survive too many days without her.

''I don't know. I just need it, Alex. So much in my life has changed.''

''Yeah,'' he said wryly. ''Mine, too.''

''I know.'' She gave him a tiny grimace and a smile. ''I'm the catalyst for most of them.''

He heard the undertone in her voice, a hint that she felt she was a negative catalyst. How could he explain to her that he needed her to fight with him against the real disastrous force that was tearing him apart—intruders fighting him for Green Forks? ''I need you, Daph.''

''No, you don't.'' She smiled, but it was a sad lift to her lips. ''I cost you what you had.''

Silence kept them apart as they stared at each other.

He could never convince her that she wasn't the reason he'd lost Green Forks. It was because of some stupid clause—and an unhappy aunt—he'd never known about. He couldn't have changed any of the past even if he had known. No doubt his powerful father had done everything he could to get the situation fixed the way he wanted. It was irretrievable—mainly, apparently, because Alexander had tried to give a younger sister the shaft, and now it was payback time.

"The only way I can see that you'll ensure Green Forks stays yours, Alex," Daphne said softly, "is for you to remarry."

Chapter Twelve

"Remarry? I have no intention of divorcing, so why should we remarry?"

"So that you can have more children." Daphne's heart shattered even as she thought about Alex with another woman. "Even though Gloria is having her son first, you are still the rightful heir to Green Forks, so your son would be next in line. If you had one."

"I don't believe I'm hearing this!" Alex shouted. "Have you lost your mind? This is not some feudal land we're talking about, a throne that belongs to a king! Henry the Eighth wed and did away with wives for the sake of gender, Daphne, but I'm just Alex Banning, married to Daphne Way and damn well going to stay that way!"

"Sh! You're going to wake the babies!" she cautioned.

"Well, I'm sorry!" he said in a husky shout. "But that was the most ridiculous thing I ever heard. Why don't you just set me up a guillotine on the back forty?"

"Oh, Alex, for heaven's sake! I didn't write the entailment clause. Your noble ancestors did!"

"Well, I'm just telling you that I'm not marrying anybody else. We had no sons. For a woman who believes in raising her children without regard to gender for any reason, you're sure buying into that bum story." He leaned on the windowsill, his frown deep in his forehead.

"What does that mean?"

"It means that for such a forward-thinking woman, you're awfully impressed with the entailment clause. Heck, you're ready to marry me off to another woman! And what happens if the second Mrs. Banning doesn't produce? Am I stuck with her, or can I divorce her and marry again? An assembly-line approach to getting the correct blue-bound bundle of joy?"

"That's not what I meant!" Daphne stiffened, hearing her reasoning on Alex's lips sound silly. It had all made sense to her. Why did he have to be so stubborn? "I just feel bad that your cousin is having a son and I can't give you one!"

He leaned back, sensing that they'd finally gotten to the source of some of Daphne's unhappiness. "Heck, Daph, if you ask me, I'd rather not have a son if it meant being married to Gloria. I mean, she looks like she's hunting for golden eggs or something. Have you seen the way she slavers every time money is mentioned? It's scary." He ran a finger over her bottom lip, which she could feel quivering. "I've never felt like you were after my money the way she appears to be after Phillip's."

"No. It was your body I wanted." She didn't dare

meet his eyes after saying that, but she had always been fiercely attracted to him.

"I know. So let me in this window."

"I can't."

Silently, he cocked a sardonic brow at her as he traced her lips.

She pulled away. "All right. I won't."

He sighed deeply, allowing his hand to fall against the windowsill. "I'll be back tomorrow night."

Her gaze was haunted when it finally rose to his. "I don't want you to pursue me, Alex." It hurt to say it, but there was so much he didn't understand!

"Okay."

He didn't sound very happy, but she didn't think she'd ever heard Alex capitulate before.

"When can I see you again?"

"I don't know." This she truly wasn't certain about. "But you can see the babies every day, if you want. Call Mom, and I'll have her send the babies with you for a couple of hours. You can send them home when they need to nurse."

He breathed deeply. "But no divorce papers."

"No. I...couldn't face that right now."

He reached out and lightly stroked the side of her face. "Sleep tight, Daph."

"I will. Good night." She slid the window shut. The curtains fell, covering it.

Alex felt as though he'd just been locked inside a prison. Resisting the urge to bang on the window and beg her not to shut him out, Alex went and got in his Mercedes.

For now, he had to face Beatrice and her group alone. It wasn't a prospect he looked forward to.

Unfortunately, as he pulled the Mercedes into the pebbled circular drive, he realized Gloria and Phillip were standing outside on the porch, as if they were waiting for someone.

They stared at him as he got out of the car. Alex eyed them over the car roof and realized they were waiting for him.

"Do you have a second, Alex?" Phillip asked as Alex strode by with a brisk nod. "Gloria and I would like to talk to you."

"I'm very busy," Alex rejoined. "What's the topic?"

Golden-haired Phillip glanced at his wife. "We know Mother's making things difficult for you."

Alex shrugged. "I've had bigger battles to fight." It was true. Losing his wife was one.

"We just want you to know we don't exactly think it's fair that she's acting this way."

Alex stared at him. What kind of son sneaked around behind his mother's back to make confessions like that? "Is there a reason you're trying to get on my good side?"

"Maybe." Phillip flicked a glance over his shoulder, as if Beatrice might appear there any moment. "Mother's damn determined to take over this ranch and run it her way. I personally don't think she's got the experience."

"And I do."

"Of course." Phillip appeared astonished that he would suggest otherwise.

"And you want to make sure the cash cow doesn't get run into the ground?" Alex narrowed his gaze on his long-lost cousin.

Phillip looked away for a moment before shrugging. "If you must put it that way, yes. Mother has no head for finances. Nor do I."

"What do you have the head for, Phillip?" Alex couldn't help asking.

Phillip glanced at Gloria as if she might know. Gloria shrugged, obviously not about to suggest anything he might be good at. A two-headed monster, Alex decided, with little brain between them.

"What do you want me to do about your mother? Can't you stand up to her yourself?" Phillip apparently lacked gut as well as brain.

"It's best not to," Phillip conceded. "But Alex, we feel caught in between on this deal. Gloria and I, well, we're on Mother's side, of course, but...but she's decided to buy ten thousand head of cattle from one of your neighbors."

"Ten thousand?" Alex repeated. His mouth fell open. "From who, may I ask?"

"Some man down south. He had an oil well he wanted to sell her, too. Mother said that if your father could buy and sell cows and make a fortune at it, she could, too."

Alex was stunned. There was no way Green Forks was equipped to handle that kind of additional load. Unfortunately, his hands were tied for the moment. "I don't know where she's going to put them all," he muttered.

Gloria and Phillip glanced at each other. "What do you mean?"

He realized they had no idea how much grazing cattle needed to do in order to be healthy. "Never mind. That's your side of the family tree at work. If that's how she wants to spend her money, that's her business." Brushing past them, he went inside.

Aunt Beatrice met him in the foyer, giving him a cool glance from under her tall hairdo. "Your father's servants are lazy," she pronounced.

"I beg your pardon?"

"Your father's servants are lazy," she repeated with gusto. "They do very little that I ask, and begrudgingly."

He found that very hard to believe of Sinclair and Nelly. Two harder-working people he had never met. "They're not servants, actually. As you might have noticed from the bequest in my father's will, he wanted them to live here as long as they wanted. They're family, as far as we're concerned."

"Maybe to you." She sniffed. "But to me they're extra mouths to feed."

He stiffened. "I'll pay their salaries and expenses out of my own funds."

"Fine. I'll find it necessary to hire my own servants, then."

"Do as you like. Please excuse me." He turned and walked away from her.

"Of course, as I expect you'll be finding other housing in the near future, I can assume they'll be going with you."

Slowly, he turned on his heel, amazed by the

change in subjects. "Nelly and Sinclair are to live here as long as they like, no matter what you sue me for."

"That silly bequest of your father's has no impact on how I run this ranch," she snapped, "particularly if they're on your payroll."

"As I don't see myself leaving my home, Beatrice, I find this whole conversation pointless." Impatiently, he left the hallway. The woman was manipulative to the bone. No doubt she had alienated the very people who could have eased her transition to the ranch. Nelly and Sinclair knew more about running Green Forks than he did.

They met him in the hallway to his father's quarters.

"Sir—"

Alex held up his hand. "I know. She's driving you nuts."

Sinclair's face held relief. "In a word, sir."

"Pay her no mind. You're on my personal payroll. You don't work for anyone but me."

"Oh, thank you," Nelly and Sinclair said.

"We've got to find a way to dislodge that canker from our backsides," he murmured. "Do you know she has bought ten thousand head of cattle?"

"They're being delivered in two weeks," Nelly informed him. "I've been listening to her conversations. 'Course, it's not difficult to do. She yells everything."

Alex looked out the window over the grounds of Green Forks. "How can that happen so quickly? It's a hell of a lot of cattle to haul."

"The man she bought them from was desperate. I heard her ask how desperate." Nelly didn't look too shamed by her eavesdropping. "She bought them at below-market price."

"I hope she hired lots of cowboys," Alex stated. "The ones we have aren't going to be able to handle the extra load."

"I hope so, too," Sinclair agreed. "Nelly and I aren't cut out for chasing stock. Your aunt already tried to get us to help the auction man inventory stuff and tag it, but we declined to do so. Suffice to say, she's rather put out with us."

"Auction man?" Alex stared at Sinclair.

"Yes." Sinclair and Nelly nodded unhappily. His trusted butler wrung his hands with worry. "I really don't know how to tell you this, Alex, but that aunt of yours said she is going to have herself 'one hell of a garage sale.'"

TWO WEEKS LATER, Daphne drove down the farm road slowly in her Suburban, the babies tucked neatly into their car seats and Danita beside her. They had very much enjoyed the drive to the quaint town square, but now they were tuckered out. Daphne had bought a new pantsuit she thought looked nice on her, the brown and bronze colors flattering. Unable to resist, she decided to drive past the Banning mansion rather than take the long way around. If she ran into Alex, she would wave and drive on with the excuse that the babies needed to get home to their cribs. He had come by regularly in the past two weeks, but she had managed to keep their visits very low-key, claiming tiredness.

She *was* tired, but more than that, she was trying to give Alex time to see that her way was the only way he could gain control of the ranch. After Beatrice's huge purchase, she knew Phillip and Gloria were right. Beatrice didn't have the first idea about running a ranch. The woman could end up costing Alex his home. Daphne couldn't bear the thought of that.

There were so many cars and stock haulers lining the road Daphne began gagging on the dust suddenly filtering in the air-conditioning vents. She drove slowly in order not to get backed into by a truck.

Daphne gasped. The scene in the pasture closest to the house stopped her completely. Steers ran everywhere, snorting their confusion. Like magnets meeting their polar opposites, they shied away from any moving thing, including the few hapless men trying to keep order. She had never seen so much cattle in one place. They had run down one long fence that separated paddocks, milling and bawling their unhappiness. In one area, a bull was trying desperately to mate with a recalcitrant female.

"Oh, my stars," Daphne whispered. "I can't believe my eyes." The babies slept quietly in the middle bench seat of the Chevy, completely uncaring of the disaster at their father's home. The ground itself looked like it had been ripped up by a furious Mother Nature.

On the walk at the top of the house, Beatrice stood watching the melee. Her arms folded across her chest, she looked pleased with the disorder, as if she were in control of everything.

Guilt tore at Daphne. She moved the Suburban forward carefully so she wouldn't accidentally hit anybody—or anything—in the crush. To her astonishment, a huge billboard had been erected at the side of the road.

Estate Auction, the sign boasted. It gave the date, one week away, when the auction would be held. A gaudy red-painted arrow pointed to the mansion. All it needed was flashing neon lights to be any more tacky.

"Oh, no," she murmured.

"Oh, no, is right," Danita agreed. "I never saw the like."

Her heart sinking, Daphne moved past the sign and the trucks and cars, hurrying home as fast as she could. She and Danita unloaded the babies, carrying them inside one by one.

Cos met them at the door, taking a baby.

"Did you see what was going on at Green Forks?" Daphne gasped.

"I did. It's a mess." Cos took the baby into the parlor and laid it out on a nice clean pallet.

"Poor Alex! He's got to be miserable!"

"I reckon so. He's lost just about everything he loved within the space of a few weeks," Danita announced as she laid a baby next to the one her husband had set out.

Daphne sent a sharp look her mother's way to see if she was trying to make a point, but Danita's face was impassive. "It's so sad! I'm sure Alexander is turning in his grave.'' She settled Alexis on the pallet, too.

''Your brothers went over to see what they could do to help. Hope they don't get themselves killed.''

Danita's tone was joking, but Daphne couldn't laugh. ''Anybody could, in that turmoil.''

''I was thinking about going over there and taking a gander at it myself,'' Cos mentioned uncertainly.

''No, you're not.'' Danita shook her head. ''You're too old to be in the middle of that cattle circus. You stay home with me and the babies, and that's quite enough activity for you.''

''I expect you're right,'' Cos agreed. His face brightened as if he was pleased to be let off the hook.

Daphne ran a hand through her hair, anguished for Alex's sake. ''I feel terrible about this! It's all my fault!''

Danita sighed and smoothed her hand over one baby's head. ''Don't fret, Daphne. That woman's gonna run that ranch into the ground because she didn't have anything on her mind other than money in the first place. But Alex'll survive.''

''I hope so.'' Daphne drooped.

''Beatrice didn't have to be such a mule, Daph. It's her choice to meddle in that which she knows nothing about. She'll learn.''

''At Alex's expense.'' Daphne couldn't help feeling responsible. No matter what anybody said, she knew what Alexander had been trying to avoid. She looked at her darling babies. She would have loved them just as much if they'd been boys. But that didn't matter, because they weren't. What mattered was that she couldn't have any more children—and that Alex had hairy beasts tearing up his inheritance. Of course, land would repair itself.

But an auction! A low-rent, tent sale auction to sell off possessions he held dear and sentimental. Beatrice was moving fast. The woman really believed Green Forks should have been hers as much as Alexander's. Though Daphne knew Beatrice might have rights at Green Forks, she hated what it was doing to Alex.

There was no fixing this problem. It just kept getting worse.

AN HOUR LATER, Alex was at the door. He was hot and sweaty and stunk to high heaven, but Danita swiftly opened the door wide so he could enter.

"Hello, Alex!" Daphne said. She wanted to hug him. He looked so tired, and so worn down.

"I met Cos coming around the back way," Alex said. "I thought I should let you know I'm inviting myself to dinner. If that's all right, I'll go down to the barn and hose off."

"Do that," Danita said. "I've got plenty of food."

Daphne's eyes drank in her husband. "Is there anything I can do?"

"I don't think so. The courts are the only ones that can straighten out my aunt."

"Well," Danita announced, "you and Daphne'll just have to get along for a spell. Alex, consider yourself at home until the dust settles. You're welcome here anytime."

Daphne glanced away from him, her blood racing.

"Thanks, Danita. Don't worry, Daphne," he said

softly. "You're safe from me. I just need to get away from the craziness for a while."

As much as she didn't want to, she understood. "Alex, I can't tell you how bad I feel. I drove by and saw what she's doing."

"It's okay." His tone said it wasn't. "I'm going to go wash." Then he strode out the door.

"Your man's hurting," Danita said.

"I know," Daphne said miserably. And he was going to hurt a lot worse before it was all over.

"I think you're letting all that will stuff tear you up, Daphne. You oughta be comfortin' your man, not keeping yourself away from him."

"I can't." Daphne's heart felt like stone settling into an uncertain low spot. The problem was, she had an announcement of her own, and she knew it wasn't going to make Alex feel one bit better.

Cos, Danita, Daphne and Alex sat at the table eating a quiet dinner thirty minutes later. Alex and Cos were quiet because they were plainly tired out from talking about the ranch. Danita was quiet because that was her nature.

Daphne was quiet because she had a load of worry on her mind. She glanced toward her father, then toward her husband and put her fork down. "Dad, I think there's something you need to tell Alex."

"Huh?" Cos reared his head like a wary bull.

Alex raised his eyebrows. Danita took a drink of tea and set the glass down, all the while keeping her eyes on Daphne.

"Like what?" Cos demanded. "Don't like jabbering at the supper table, Daphne Way. You know that.''

But his eyes glinted at her with unquestionable suspicion.

''Tell him about the cows.'' It was killing her inside. She yearned to know he had not done what she had heard about on her shopping foray. Maybe it was all a terrible rumor.

''Daughter, we've done all the talking about cows that's gonna be done in this family,'' he asserted sternly. ''Get back to eating your supper and leave me to mine.''

Alex watched her steadily. She saw the concern in his blue eyes and couldn't stand it another moment. ''Dad! You have to tell him!''

Cos threw down his dinner napkin, his expression disgusted as he met Alex's gaze. ''Oh, all right,'' he said with too much bravado, ''I reckon Daphne's upset because of a silly little woman thing. She's obviously heard that the rancher your aunt Beatrice bought those steers from was a family member of ours.''

''A family member?'' Alex looked at Daphne, then back to Cos. Danita's hand fell into her lap as she gave up the calm facade. ''What family member?''

''Well, it's like this.'' Cos relaxed in the old ladder-back chair, as if he had a story to tell that was complicated. ''You remember Uncle Bob, don'tcha?''

''I certainly do. I bought the Chevy from him for Daphne.''

''Yep. Well, he'd been down playing bingo with some of the boys and learned that one of our brothers had overseen himself in the cattle market. That would be Daphne's uncle Herman.''

"Oh, Cos," Danita said.

Cos waved her silent. "Now, I know it sounds bad. But you gotta see the way I was thinking. Your aunt Beatrice was of a mind to be spending her money on something she knew nothing about. Herman hit a bad patch in the futures market and needed to sell his stock. Prices are undervalued right now, you know," he said to Alex, as if Alex wouldn't have been abreast of the cattle market himself, "and he knew he wouldn't get much for draggin 'em up to auction. So I told him to call your aunt Beatrice," he said, puffing out his chest and mighty proud of his tale.

Alex stared at Cos. He looked as though he couldn't believe his ears. Danita threw her napkin on the table. "Are you saying you laundered overpriced cattle through Alex's citified aunt Beatrice just so Herman could have a naive buyer with ready cash?"

"Now, Danita, you don't exactly unnerstand—"

"I do understand! Oh, Cos! How could you?" Shooting a sorrowful glance at Alex, she said, "When are you ever going to learn to leave well enough alone?"

Cos stared at her, then at Daphne.

"Oh, Dad," she murmured. "I was hoping it wasn't true. Do you have any idea what you've done?"

"What? What did I do?" Cos cried, apparently overwhelmed by the face of blame everyone at his table was wearing.

"You've made everything worse, that's what

you've done,'' Daphne said. She couldn't meet Alex's eyes. Shame burned all over her, like nettles on her skin. Her daddy really was a cheat, as Alexander had claimed all along. He was obviously just out to get whatever he could from the Bannings. It made her feel like a peddler's daughter. ''The only thing that could make this whole thing more sorry is if you were the one who gave Aunt Beatrice the bright idea to have her infamous garage sale.'' Daphne stared at the old lace tablecloth under the white dinner plate with faded flowers. She could feel Alex's confusion—and his eyes on her.

''Well,'' Cos said slowly, ''I reckon ya'll are gonna be mad at me about this, too, then, but I heard at the barbershop that Beatrice had called down to Framall's Auction about getting someone to run her estate sale.'' He glanced around the table, measuring the effect of his announcement. ''So when I heard that, 'course I called brother Billy in Waco to let him know he should put in a bid on the business. He's a real-live auctioneer, ya know,'' he said to Alex.

Daphne jumped from her chair and rushed from the room.

''Oh, Cos.'' Danita sighed. ''Your daughter is never going to forgive you.''

Chapter Thirteen

Alex immediately excused himself from the dinner table and went down the hall after Daphne. No doubt he wasn't welcome, but she was his wife. She wasn't going to cry if he could help it.

She lay on the bed, golden-bronze hair spilling across the pillow, one hand resting on her forehead. Tears streamed down her face as she silently wept.

He couldn't stand it.

"Daphne," he murmured, sitting next to her on the bed. "I wish you wouldn't allow small things to upset you."

"It's not small to me," she whispered. "I'm so ashamed."

Pulling her into his arms as he leaned against the headboard, he said, "I know what you're thinking, but what Cos did isn't all that bad. At least not to me."

"That's because your father didn't spend every day of his life trying to think of a way to weasel a deal!"

"The hell he didn't." He closed his eyes, enjoying the feel of Daphne in his arms, unresisting. "It's a sure bet he spent twice as much time on it as Cos and was twice as productive. Beatrice isn't hopping mad for nothing.''

"She's greedy.''

"I don't know.'' Alex frowned. "I'd like to know why Dad was so selfish with her. We both know Dad bought into that feudal attitude, but the truth is, even he had to know Beatrice was entitled to something.'' He shifted, realizing Daphne's head against his waist was arousing him. "I'm real uncomfortable with the thought he was paying her off. At least you can't say that about Cos. His mind may always be working when it comes to money, but he's always thinking of a way to benefit the many members of his clan.''

"We don't know that your father was paying Beatrice off.'' Daphne stared at him with large green eyes as her chin rested on his chest.

"I've been going through Dad's personal effects, trying to piece the real story together. So far, I've found a few checks with her name on them, but no personal correspondence.''

"Why would he treat his sister that way?''

"I don't know.'' Alex ran a slow, caressing hand through Daphne's soft hair again and again, the feel of it soothing. "Unless he truly believed he was protecting the ranch for me. When the original will from my grandparents is located, that should tell the whole tale. But I have a funny feeling Beatrice knows she's got reason to be furious.''

"She still doesn't have the right to hold an estate sale without your permission.'' Daphne raised her chin, angrily defiant for his sake.

He smiled at her. "A letter from my lawyer put a stop to that quick enough."

"Really?"

"Oh, yeah. She's a fast mover, but I don't get caught off guard too easily, Daph. Green Forks is my home, and she's not selling anything without my okay. Family or not, I'll shower her with legal papers if she keeps on the way she is. As it is, we're countersuing her claims to the estate to slow her down so we can figure out exactly what she's entitled to, and whether we can work a deal with her. Could be that all she wants is money." Privately, he didn't think so. She'd sounded determined to live at the ranch and run cattle.

As if that was all there was to it.

"What are you going to do about all those steers she bought?" Daphne's worried gaze stayed on his.

"Nothing." He snorted, exasperated. "It's her money. Maybe that rodeo she's got going on over there will keep her too busy to mess up anything else. I need her preoccupied so I can give the lawyer time to develop a strategy. And I've got to look through Dad's papers for anything that might help my case."

"But Beatrice is tearing up Green Forks! How can you bear to see the damage she's doing to the ranch?"

"I can't," he replied grimly. "But I'd rather work on fixing other things. Right now, Beatrice and her cattle are the least of my worries."

Truth to tell, his marriage worried him far more. He sighed and closed his eyes, wondering what it would take for life to get back to the way it had been before.

He wanted Daphne and his children under his roof—and Beatrice and her crew far away.

It was a goal he was determined to achieve.

"I CAN'T STAND IT," Phillip said to Gloria. "That constant mooing and bellowing every minute of the day is about to drive me out of my mind."

The restless steers could distinctly be heard in their bedroom. Gloria and Phillip had been given a room on the lower floor, which looked out on a paddock. No doubt the view was usually peaceful and pastoral, but with his mother's dramatic delivery of prime rib on hooves, the noise was worse than New York City on a Saturday night.

"I think she bought too many," Gloria said worriedly. "They don't all seem to fit very well in their yard."

"Corral, Gloria." He rubbed a hand wearily through his shiny blond hair. "Damn it! I know buying in quantity is usually the way to get the best deal, but Mother went over the top with those animals. No doubt she's sleeping in relative quiet in her room while we get treated to the Bovine Chorus." He shot a resentful glance in the direction of Beatrice's room.

"I don't see what stewing about it is going to get you." Gloria giggled. "Get it? Stew?"

He was in no mood to joke about the stew beef roaming outside. A particularly loud moo came from nearby, sounding almost in the bedroom with them. He crossed to the window and looked out into a pair of questioning brown eyes. "Damn it! They've gotten out of the corral!"

Gloria ran to the window. "Oh, it's slobbering on the window! Shoo it away, Phillip! It's looking at me!"

He couldn't decide which party should be more frightened, Gloria or the cow. His wife wore no makeup and had plastic curlers the size of hot dogs in her hair. She'd been in the process of gluing in some extra eyelashes, so she appeared lopsided. The glamor she exuded during the day definitely did not extend to her nightly routine.

"You're looking at it, too," he said reasonably. "Gloria, it can't hurt you. It's just a harmless cow."

The cow turned its head, banging the window abruptly with a large horn. Gloria screamed.

"Sh!" Phillip commanded. "Don't get it more excited than it already is." Clearly the animal wasn't any happier to be out of the corral than they were to have it spying on them. "I'll go see if I can convince the silly thing not to stare in our window all night."

Sighing heavily, he pulled on a pair of expensive loafers.

"Shouldn't you call the local animal control office?" Gloria demanded worriedly. "That thing is enormous."

"It's just a cow, Gloria. Worst-case scenario, I'll get a little cow poo on my shoes."

"Ugh. Don't wear them back inside if you do. Sinclair and Nelly aren't much for cleaning, and I don't want to have to get down on my hands and knees and clean that marble entry. I'm pregnant, and cleaning solutions, never mind cow poo, are harmful to a fetus."

Pregnancy or no, cleaning solutions of any kind would toxify Gloria. His wife had two maids for their small, exclusive town house in Philly. "I'm sure a little Ajax wouldn't hurt the baby, but I'll be careful."

He went outside and headed to the front of the house.

"Go on," he told the cow.

It turned its great head to stare at him. He could see the whites of large, wide-open eyes. Best he could tell, the body portion appeared to be of good size. He reached inside the door to turn on the porch light so he could see better. "Well, go on," he repeated, flapping his hands. "Get back in your corral."

His jaw dropped as the creature began a ponderous walk toward him. From the light in the bedroom window, he could see Gloria's mouth become a worried O. At this moment, Phillip was feeling none too confident himself.

"Nice cow," he said, backing up. "Now you be a good cow and go back and join your friends."

For some reason, the cow began a swift trot toward him. It clattered onto the porch, its hooves clapping like thunder on the brick.

It was coming right at him. Phillip jerked the glass door open just in time to jump into the house.

Unfortunately, a great, long horn managed to get caught between the glass door and the doorjamb.

"Moo!" the cow bellowed.

"Holy smokes!" Phillip shrieked.

"Get it out of the house!" Gloria screamed from behind him.

"How?"

The animal let out another earsplitting, moaning moo. Gloria screamed again.

"Shut up!" Phillip yelled at her. "I can't think with you doing that!"

His wife fled. He heard their bedroom door slam. The cow tossed its head, working itself further into the house. Phillip backed up cautiously.

"Now look here, Mr. Cow. You don't really want in here, and I really don't want you in here. So get your head out of my door and everybody will be a lot happier, don't you agree?"

The animal's horns banged against the glass. Phillip gasped, wondering if the door would shatter. For the moment it was holding, but he didn't know how much longer that would be the case.

"You're being quite the ruffian, but if you'll go on like a good cow, I'll forget about this incident. If you don't, it's the grill for you," he warned.

The cow gave another great shake of its horns, and Phillip realized it was stuck.

He was going to have to touch the awful thing in order to free it if he ever wanted the horned door fixture returned to its pasture.

"What in heaven's name is going on?"

His mother's vexed voice startled Phillip so badly he jumped a foot. "Mother! Must you creep about?"

"Really, Phillip! What is a bull doing in the house?"

"Bull?" He turned to stare at the beast. "Bull?"

"Yes. A bull. You act like you've never seen one before," she said impatiently.

He was fairly certain he hadn't, and certainly not one determined to get in a house he was occupying.

"Move," she commanded. Like a soldier of war, his mother approached the bull, took hold of its horn and gave it a shove. Either from shock or because she'd freed it, the massive head disappeared from the doorway. The glass door slammed shut, but the animal remained on the porch staring at them.

"Turn off the light, ninny!" she instructed her son. "Unless you want him standing out there all night."

Phillip jumped to do her bidding. The hallway went dark, but the bull, obviously perplexed, continued standing on the porch.

"I don't think he can hurt anything out there now." Beatrice firmly closed the heavy wooden door behind the glass one. "The cowboys will be up soon. They'll get the bull back to his place."

She turned toward her room. Phillip stared, his jaw dropping. "Mother, there could be others roaming around out there. You wouldn't want any of your purchases wandering off down the road."

"You're right. I'll call the bunkhouse."

She went off, comfortable with her decision. He was not, but he preferred to leave the whole dilemma in his mother's hands.

Phillip went to his room, knowing he had an upset wife on the other side of the door. Even if his mother was in her element, he was definitely not in his by any stretch. He could hear Gloria weeping, which she did a lot of since she'd become pregnant. He sighed self-pityingly.

Living the life of a wealthy cattle baron was hard on his nerves.

"I want to go home to Philly!" Gloria wailed when he opened the door. The hot dog curlers were askew. One group of false eyelashes had come unglued. They clumped, waving like pointy spider legs, from the top of an eyelid.

Getting home to Philly seemed like a distant dream. He wanted the same thing his wife did.

Unfortunately, his mother would have a fit if he left. "Argh!" he groaned to nobody in particular. His disastrously weepy wife gasped, peering out the window where the bull had returned to look in.

It was going to be a long night.

"DISGRACEFUL!" Beatrice scolded him the next morning. From their end of the breakfast table, Gloria and Phillip glanced up. "I never saw such useless behavior in all my life." She buttered toast with an angry swipe. "You, Gloria, caterwauling like an upset infant. And Phillip, were you just going to leave that animal stuck in the door all night?"

"I would have thought of something," he said defensively. "Sooner or later." Shooting a stern stare at Gloria to tell her to keep quiet, he decided pacifying his mother was the best route to making sure he stayed on her good side. "I think the cattle you bought were a wise investment."

Beatrice eyed him narrowly. "Do you?"

"Of course. Why not?"

Beatrice shrugged, trying to appear nonchalant.

"Alex mentioned he thought I'd perhaps bought too many."

"Oh, please." Phillip picked up his glass of orange juice. "Alex is going to say anything to make you feel like you don't know what you're doing." He started to sip his juice. Gloria pinched the inside of his thigh, making him gasp with pain and choke.

"Maybe you did buy a couple too many," Gloria began, whacking Phillip on the back, "just one or two, I'm sure, Beatrice. You could run an ad in the paper and sell off a few. Or even during the garage sale you could mention you got a couple of extra...how do they say it? Heads of cattle to sell."

"I can't have the garage sale," Beatrice complained. Her lips puckered with annoyance. "Alex has filed an injunction against me."

"What?" Phillip put his glass down. "He can't do that."

"Tell that to a rinky-dink small-town judge who's known him since he was in diapers." She abruptly leaned back in the chair, her dress sleeves puffing out. "It's going to be hard to turn this place around. It'll be a real battle to make it what it should be. But I'm determined." She laid a many-ringed hand on the damask tablecloth. "This place is going to be a showplace, a jewel unrivaled by the Astor or Vanderbilt estates, if it's the last thing I do on this earth."

Phillip didn't know what to say to that. He had a funny feeling Alex would have plenty to say, though. Nervously, he checked his watch. Any second now he expected his cousin to appear at the breakfast table. Not that he would ever admit it, but he admired cousin Alex. The man was everything he was not: Tall, powerfully built, annoyingly commanding. Formidable, and not the least bit concerned about standing up to Beatrice. Phillip wished he could do that. He was soft-spoken, slightly built and not made for confrontation, whether with his mother or curious cows.

It was a bull, he reminded himself. He wouldn't have been intimidated by a simple cow.

Alex walked in and seated himself at the head of the table. He nodded briefly to Beatrice at the opposite end.

She set her fork down, her eyes gleaming with what Phillip recognized as her battle expression.

"Alex, I was just telling Phillip about my plans for Green Forks."

Alex appeared unruffled. "It's a bit soon for you to be making plans of any kind, Beatrice."

"Still, one must always prepare for the future. And I want the best for Green Forks." She leaned forward, her enthusiasm taking hold of her. "We need to make modifications. I intend to sell the cattle off at a profit in time, and then I want to open the ranch to wealthy visitors, a place where even Robin Leach will want to run an episode of 'Lifestyles of the Rich and Famous.' Only the best, of course." Smiling, she said, "Can you imagine Tom Cruise and his wife staying here?"

Phillip couldn't. Gloria stared at Beatrice as if she'd sprouted another head.

Alex shrugged. "Don't count your movie stars before they arrive, Beatrice."

"We'll be known far and wide for our tasteful, genteel hospitality." With a satisfied smile, she leaned back. "Of course, we're going to have to get rid of a lot of the junk that's accumulated during my brother's, ah, reign at the helm of Green Forks."

Alex gave her a jaundiced stare before taking a drink of coffee. "Do you think tasteful and genteel is something you could imitate, Beatrice?"

She sat back, highly affronted. "How dare you?"

"I'm not daring. I'm making an observation. From your behavior since you've been here, I wasn't sure you were acquainted with the definition of those words."

She tossed her napkin onto the table. "Alex, we don't have to get along to live under the same roof."

"No, we don't." He shrugged languidly. "I'm not planning on it, actually."

Gloria burst into tears. "I can't live under this kind of strain!"

Phillip patted her hand. "It's okay, dear."

"Get a grip, Gloria," Beatrice commanded. "Everything in life is not a one-act play with you as the star."

Gloria sucked in a breath, insulted, and fled the room.

Phillip watching his crying wife's exit with concern. He turned, catching Alex's gaze on him. His cousin had him pinned with a relentless stare, almost as if he were waiting for his move. What was it that Alex was waiting for?

His mother calmly buttered a biscuit as if nothing was wrong. He turned to Alex.

Phillip knew what he had to do. After listening to Alex battle with Beatrice, he could do it, too.

"Mother, I don't think you should talk to Gloria that way," he began cautiously.

"Why not? Someone has to snap that girl into line when she allows herself to cry all the time."

He took a deep breath and slowly stood. "If you don't mind, Mother, I think Gloria's had all the snapping in she can take from you."

"Watch your mouth, Phillip." His mother stabbed the air with the butter knife. "Your allowance comes out of my purse, remember."

His face burned with shame. The statement, though humiliating, was true. His entire life-style depended on his mother. "Still, I think you owe her an apology."

"I owe her nothing. Sit down and finish your breakfast."

He started to sit before he realized it. "No, thanks," he said, backing away from the table in jerky motions. He caught his chair before it hit the floor. "I'm not hungry."

Without further hesitation, he, too, made a fast exit.

Alex stared down the table at Beatrice. "Your troops are deserting you."

She gave him a nasty look. "So? Yours left a few weeks ago. This is between you and me, anyway. I don't need backup."

Alex forbore to comment, but he was struck by incredible realization. Gloria was crying because she felt out of place. Though it was Cos's wheeling and dealing that had set off Daphne's crying last night, the pressure had built because she felt out of place in Alex's life. Beatrice had a point. His troops *had* deserted him. But only because Daphne thought he didn't need her. She felt like the lesser half of their relationship.

He needed her.

The answer was obvious. He'd been going at this situation all wrong. He wanted Daphne under his roof, but the crucial point was Daphne and his family, not necessarily location. No doubt his aunt would turn the ranch into the Graceland of Texas, but he didn't care. Whatever it took, he intended to convince his wife they belonged together.

He was leaving.

Chapter Fourteen

Alex told Nelly and Sinclair where he was heading. Then he tossed a bag of clothes into the Mercedes and headed down the road toward the Way household.

Cos met him at the door. "What are you doing?" he demanded, eyeing Alex's bag.

"Coming to stay with my family." Alex waited, wondering if Cos would run him off. Suddenly, he knew how Cos had felt all these years, too proud to ask for help of any kind. So he'd resorted to crafty maneuvers to get around Alexander, who'd been a fairly imposing king of the hill.

Alex took note of this lesson and softened his approach. "If it's all right with you," he amended.

"Fine by me," Cos said, opening the door wide, "I'd rather have ya in the house than sneaking about at all hours. But you gotta get my daughter's permission."

"Hello, Alex," Danita said, walking into the small entry with a baby bottle. "Going somewhere?"

"Here, if you'll have me."

Danita handed him the bottle. "You'd best go talk

it over with your family. You'll find them down the hall.''

''Thanks.'' He began to head that way.

''Alex.'' Cos's voice stopped him.

''Yes?'' He turned to look at his host.

''I...uh...'' Cos scratched his head, skewing the little bit of hair he had. His lanky body hunched over. ''I'm sorry about that earlier business.''

''Oh.'' Alex knew he meant the business that had upset Daphne last night. ''Cos, that's between you and Daphne.''

''Naw, it's 'tween you and me.'' Cos stood a little straighter. ''Truth is, I've grown accustomed to trying to take advantage of your father. And Daphne's right. I had no right to try to make family profit off of your misfortune. I apologize.'' He ducked his head. Danita reached out and caught her husband's hand in hers. ''I hope you'll not think the less of me for it.''

Alex felt sorry for the old man. ''It means a lot to me that you see the difference between my father and me, Cos. I'd like to have a different kind of relationship with you,'' he said, reaching out to shake Cos's hand, ''particularly as I'm part of your family now.'' He nodded as Cos returned his handshake. ''And I plan on staying in the family. I wouldn't mind having you in my corner.''

Cos appeared shocked by the thought of Alex being a part of his family as opposed to being on the other side of enemy lines. Danita smiled gently at him, but Alex could almost hear the thoughts churning in old Cos's mind.

''I hadn't thought of it thataway,'' Cos said slowly.

"I've been seeing some things in a new light lately myself." A wail sounded from down the hall. Alex held up the baby bottle. "I'm being summoned."

Cos nodded, still apparently considering Alex's words. Alex turned toward Daphne's room. She had the three little babies spread out on blankets engaged in various activities—crying, looking around and sucking on fists.

"What are you doing?" she asked, putting her hands on her hips when she saw Alex.

"I know you said you weren't ready to decide about our marriage, but…" Alex faltered as he stared into his wife's lovely green eyes. "I hope you'll reconsider. Beatrice is a crazy woman, and if I don't stay with you, I'll have to go to a hotel."

She stared at him, her expression unyielding.

"Of course, that's actually an excuse, and not a very good one." He set down the bottle and the bag but didn't go near Daphne. Something told him his wife was waiting to hear something—and touching her right now would be a mistake. "I can stay in a hotel. I just don't want to. I need you, and I need my children. I miss my family."

Her expression softened a bit. Hope rose inside Alex.

"It's no good hiding out here," she told him. "You're always welcome, Alex, to see the children." Taking a deep breath, she said, "But you being here would negate what I was trying to give you back by leaving you. And you can't allow Beatrice to push you into running away."

"I'm not. I'm running to my wife, and that's different."

"Alex, you don't understand—"

"I do. I really think I do. You're upset because you think you should have had a boy." He pointed to the blankets spread out with babies squirming in pink diapers and little dresses. "Can you really look at these little ladies and tell me you'd be happier if they were boys?"

"No," Daphne replied, shaking her head, "but you're the one with an entailment clause hanging over you."

"Yes, and it was my chromosomes that chose the sex for those three little people. Daphne, I'm just so surprised at your behavior. You've always told me how important it is that girls and boys are treated the same. Why aren't you living what you preach?"

"I am!" Her eyes blazed with helpless anger. "Alex, it's too hard! The whole situation is all wrong. It was set up from the start—"

"No, it wasn't!" he roared. "Woman, you just don't want to listen!"

The babies started crying in unison. Daphne instantly bent to scoop one up, as did Alex.

"You can't stay here. We don't see eye to eye on this matter," she told him over the top of Danielle's head.

"I want to stay," he insisted. "Either I do, or I want you to come with me," he informed her over Alexis's head. "Quite frankly, I think you're chicken, which I find very odd in a woman who had triplets without a moment's doubt."

"I'm not chicken!"

"Prove it." He slipped the bottle into Alexis's mouth. She quieted instantly, her waving fist stilling on his chest. Despite the turmoil of his marital situation, a strange and wonderful peace filled him. He decided there was almost no better feeling in the world than trusting baby fingers resting against his heart.

"I don't have to prove anything." Supremely annoyed with him, Daphne sat on the edge of the bed and opened her shirt to Danielle. Alex's eyes popped open appreciatively.

"No, you don't, but so far, I think I'm the only one who's been trying to compromise, Daphne. As your mother says, divorce is bad economy when there's three little children involved. I realize you've got a lot going on right now, but I do think you could at least meet me halfway."

Her head drooped. "Alex, you don't understand."

"Try me."

She took a deep breath, cradling her child to her as she held his gaze. "Okay. As silly as it sounds—and as irrational as it might be—it's terribly difficult for me that Gloria is giving birth to a son."

There. She'd said it. The terrible fear was out in the open.

She'd kill Alex if he made light of it.

"Daphne," he said slowly, "you're a bigger person than that."

"I know it!" she wailed. "But I can't help the way I feel."

He inched closer. "You're letting a bunch of little

stuff build up to one big stop sign in our marriage. The sign should read yield, honey.''

''I know you're right,'' she whispered. ''But I'm always going to feel like I didn't do what I was expected to. And it makes it worse that Gloria can.''

''Well, I don't care about Gloria and whatever babies she and Phillip have.'' He nuzzled Alexis's hand when it reached toward his nose. ''I'm staying here with my own, Daphne. I'm not letting you toss me out. You'll just have to accept that I'm the one who needs something this time.''

She couldn't believe that. He had money, power, good looks.

''Alex, it's not the same.''

''It is. I have no roof over my head, no food on the table and no family to help me. I'm starting over from the beginning like everybody else.''

''With just several million to make your struggle a little less painful,'' she reminded him. Still, her ears heard the magical promise he was making. *He* needed *her*. And she had to admit that his determination to keep their marriage together was deliciously appealing. She had thought, given the easy way out, he might reconsider the wisdom of them staying together.

It had sounded so sensible to her. He should move on and father children with a woman of wealth and breeding like himself.

She had lived in agonizing fear that he would do so.

''Alex,'' she murmured, moving Danielle to her

crib before picking up Sabrina, "come sit over here. There's something I want to tell you."

He got up and approached the bed with the now sleeping Alexis in his arms. "No, you don't, sweetie," he told the baby, "we get the burp, and then we sleep."

She obliged him loudly when he gently lifted her to his chest. "Whew, this one's a stevedore," he commented.

Alexis never opened her eyes. Daphne watched with a proud smile as her husband laid the baby in her crib. Her heart beat faster as he came to sit beside her, watching her feed Sabrina with great interest.

"I'd like to help with that." His gaze hungrily moved over Daphne's breast.

"I don't think you can." Daphne's pulse picked up at the warmth flaring in her husband's eyes.

"You don't imagine she'll share, do you?"

She softly laughed at the hopeful tone in his voice. "I don't think you want any of this."

"I've never been a man to turn my nose up at new foods. I believe in trying a little bit of everything."

His eyebrows lifted wickedly before he lowered his head to the breast Sabrina wasn't occupying. He gently licked Daphne's sensitized nipple. She thought she might die from all the sexual desire suddenly flooding her body. "Oh, Alex," she half moaned, half whispered.

Very gently, he cupped her breast in his hand, laving the nipple with his tongue. Her husband and her baby needing her, drinking from her, put tears in Daphne's eyes. "Stop," she murmured.

He lifted his head. "Why?"

"Because I can't take it," she said honestly. "I want to make love with you so badly it hurts."

She closed her eyes as he placed butterfly kisses all over the smooth flesh of her breast. "I'm trying to be a patient man, but I don't think it's working."

She felt glad, but sad, too. "I don't think I'm emotionally ready." Her eyelids lowered. "I'm sorry, Alex."

"It's okay." He lay on the bed, pulling her against him so he could hold her. "I'm not trying to rush you, impatient as I feel. I do want to hold you, every minute I can." He snuggled into the curve of her neck, his breath warm against her flesh. "I promised Sinclair I wouldn't drag you home again, and you see that I'm restraining myself."

She had to smile. "It's going to be really difficult if we're living together," she warned him lightly. "Do you think we can live under the same roof and not...you know?"

"We never have before," he reminded her.

She had to laugh at the truth of that.

"But I can handle a little deprivation. If it means you'll let me stay, I'm up to the challenge. I'm willing to wait until you're ready."

She got up to burp Sabrina and put her in a crib, bundling her nicely for her nap. Then she walked over and pulled Alex to a sitting position.

"That's not what I had in mind," she told him. "I meant *your* roof."

He hesitated, shocked, as he looked into her eyes. "Do you mean you're coming back to Green Forks?"

His voice was so hoarse with hope that Daphne felt rewarded. "I might have to," she said softly, "I don't like my husband thinking I'm too chicken to face up to his family." Taking his face between her hands, she said, "You know, I handled Alexander just fine. Surely I can manage his sister."

"And Gloria?"

That caused a spear to go through her heart. "I'll put my jealousy in its place."

He put his hands over hers. "That's the spirit. That's the woman I married."

"Really?"

"Of course. My dad knew what he was doing when he picked you out."

She yelped and beat his back with her fists. "Alex Banning!" she cried, laughing.

He pulled her against him. "If I'd known the way to get to you was through your pride, I would have said it days ago. Chicken, chicken, chicken." He caught her lips with his so she couldn't rebut his statement.

They kissed for several long moments. When they both needed breath, Daphne had her reply ready. "It's just that I can't stand to see my husband retreat. If he lacks backbone, then I shall be his spine."

"Good woman," he murmured underneath her chin, obviously undeterred by her barb.

She could feel his interest in her growing as he held her. No wonder he wasn't responding to her teasing! He had something far more interesting on his mind. It was so tempting to relax into his arms and find the comfort that they'd once shared in each other....

A loud creaking and splintering of wood, followed by a terrifying racket that sounded like a thousand hooves descending on the house, made her sit up straight in Alex's lap. She jumped to her feet. "What in heaven's name is that?"

Alex shot down the hall to peer out the north window. Daphne followed, her eyes wide at the disaster heading their way.

"Cos!" Alex shouted. "Cattle stampede!"

"I KNEW this was going to happen!" Phillip shouted at his mother. "You bought too many cows!"

Daphne, Cos and Alex stood watching as a curtain of dust puffed into the air, borne on the fury of the charging, departing herd. Daphne and the two men had hurried to the mansion in the Suburban to see if they could help—and to make certain no one had been trampled.

The damage was done. The cattle had taken to their hooves and overrun one of the south fences to make their escape. A few animals had scattered to the pastureland nearest the house, where a gate swung open awkwardly as if someone had forgotten to close it. A bull watched from inside the corral, not making an effort to leave with the herd. It kept its attention focused on the humans standing in the front yard.

Gloria hovered to one side, pale in the summer's heat, silent as her husband berated his mother. But Beatrice stood tall and full of bravado against the anger her son cast at her.

"You'll never make a rancher," Beatrice told him. "You didn't secure the gate chain after you finally convinced that lovesick bull to get back into the corral. It's no surprise to me that any of this has happened! You didn't want to come here in the first place, and you're sabotaging my efforts! Well, who do you think I'm doing all this for, anyway? You!'' she shouted, with a finger pointed squarely at him.

"You're doing it for yourself,'' he stated, "and wrecking the ranch in the process.''

He took a deep breath, glancing at the assembled group. In the distance, yelling could be heard as the hands tried to work the cattle off the road and onto Banning ranch land where they could eventually be fenced. Phillip's eyes met Daphne's briefly, and she lowered her gaze in sympathy. Nobody knew better than she how difficult it was to face up to Banning expectations—and fall short.

"I'm leaving,'' he announced suddenly. He pinned his gaze to Alex. "I'm not cut out for this.''

"You're not going anywhere.'' Beatrice put her hands on her hips in an aggressive stance.

He shot her a narrow look that didn't brook argument. "I am. I'm going home, and Gloria's going with me.''

Nobody said a word for several seconds. Daphne watched her husband to see how he would take his cousin's pronouncement. Would he be glad to see Phillip go? Though they should have been at odds because of Beatrice's determined encroachment of Alex's home, Daphne had sensed that Alex would have liked to get to know his cousin better. Beatrice, of course, had made a friendship between the two men highly unlikely.

Beatrice turned to the weaker of her two cohorts. "Gloria?" she asked silkily.

That one word was potent with threat. Daphne sensed that money was at stake now, the income Phillip and Gloria were used to living on in danger of being cut off if she didn't convince her husband to stay at Green Forks.

"*Are* you going back to Philly, Gloria?" Beatrice inquired.

A very wan Gloria hesitated one second before speaking. "Actually, no," she whispered, perspiration shining on her top lip. "I believe I'll go to the hospital." She looked suddenly at Daphne. "Help me," she moaned, before sagging into her husband's arms.

Chapter Fifteen

Before she realized what she was doing, Daphne loaded Phillip and Gloria into the Suburban. The large vehicle was comfortable for Gloria, who needed room to lie down and curl up. She did, moaning, with a worried Phillip rubbing her back.

Cold sweat broke out on Daphne's shoulders. She was relieved when Alex took the keys from her hand.

"I'll drive. You get in," he directed.

She was happy to let him take the wheel. She hadn't thought he would want to accompany them to the hospital. That thought was unworthy of Alex, though. He had always been willing to help anyone who needed it.

"I don't want to have my baby in this backwater," Gloria moaned from the back seat. "Phillip, I want to go home! I want to have my baby in a real hospital, not one with a bunch of hicks touching me and seeing me…bare!"

Daphne tried not to smile. She recognized the anxiety wrapping itself in Gloria's mind. First-time childbirth was frightening! She'd had to do it without Alex when there was nothing more that she would have liked than having him by her side.

Glancing at his profile as he backed up the vehicle, leaving a surprised, frozen Beatrice behind, Daphne made herself forget the past. What had happened was over. What mattered now was Gloria and Phillip.

She turned in the seat to meet Gloria's eyes. "Gloria, I just had three babies in the local hospital. If they can assist my delivery competently, they'll be able to take care of yours just fine," she said, her tone calm and soothing.

Gloria's face contorted as another spasm hit. "I didn't mean to call you guys hicks," she said on a groan. "I don't know what I meant."

"I know you didn't mean that, and I didn't take it that way," Daphne said. Alex's hand stole across the seat to clasp her hand in his, and Daphne's heart swelled. *He was proud of her.* "You'll be very pleased with the care you get in town, so let that be the last thing on your mind. Concentrate on your breathing," she instructed.

"I can't!" Gloria wailed. Her frightened, pained gaze met Daphne's. "It's happening, isn't it?"

There wasn't any way to get around that one, Daphne decided. For the first time, she felt sorry for Gloria. In spite of all her airy ways, she was no different than any other woman going through childbirth—except that she was a bit more unprepared for it than someone more practical might have been. "I'm not a doctor, Gloria, so I can't be sure, but you seem to be suffering similar contractions," she said sympathetically.

"These aren't contractions!" Gloria shouted. "It's pain!"

"Can't you drive faster, Alex?" Phillip asked anxiously. His skin was whiter than normal for a man who spent no time outdoors. There wasn't a spare inch of room between him and his wife on the bench seat because he was pressed so close to her.

He loves her, Daphne realized. *He really does.* She had no idea why that pleased her so much, except that maybe it was nice to know everyone in the family hadn't inherited Beatrice's cold heart. It made knowing that Alex was driving the future heir to Green Forks to the hospital a little easier to bear, somehow. She squeezed her husband's fingers, and he sent a tight smile her way.

"I'm going a moderate ten miles over the speed limit, Phillip. It's just three blocks more, so try to hang on."

Daphne admired Alex's strength. He was a good man! Why couldn't things have been different for them? Why couldn't they have been plain old Alex and Daphne in the country somewhere with no family lands and feuds hanging over their marriage?

"Breathe, Gloria," Daphne instructed, "like this." And as she proceeded to show Gloria how to relax, Daphne caught Alex glancing her way questioningly, and suddenly she knew what was on his mind.

He was paying attention to what she had gone through just a few weeks before.

A stark realization hit her. He was wondering what it would have been like to have been there for the birth of his own children. And if he stayed married to her, it was a life experience, a miracle he would never know.

She had stolen from him.

Like her daddy.

TWO HOURS LATER, Daphne realized with a sinking heart that Gloria's delivery wasn't going well. The woman wasn't comfortable, she'd lost her ability to concentrate, and Phillip was in worse shape than his wife.

"I'm going to have to leave to nurse the babies," Daphne told Alex. She stared at him, distraught. "I hate to leave you here, but I think Phillip needs you."

Alex shook his head. "I'd better drive you home."

Shaken by a newfound sense of guilt over what she'd done to her husband, Daphne touched his cheek softly. "I'm sorry, Alex," she whispered.

He caught her hand in his gently. "For what?"

"For robbing you of the chance to see your babies being born."

A hoarse cry of pain erupted from inside the birthing room. Alex jerked his head toward the sound. "Was that Gloria or Phillip?"

"I'm not sure." Daphne's worried gaze darted to her husband.

"I'm just sorry you went through this alone, if this is what childbirth is all about. I should have been there with you." His voice was so distressed that Daphne felt terrible.

"I was way too stubborn about the whole thing. I...I—well, never mind. I suppose it's water under the bridge now."

"Was it like this for you?" Alex asked hesitantly.

"Actually, no." Daphne shook her head. "They seem to be suffering quite a bit more than I did. I do hope nothing's wrong." It was a worry that kept running through her mind. "Since I had a Cesarean, my delivery went more smoothly. Gloria and Phillip are going through an entirely different process."

A process she wasn't sure was on-track for a successful delivery. Gloria was physically exhausted after only eight hours of labor. It had progressed rapidly, and then slowed to a grinding halt. The doctor had been in to see Gloria, and he appeared comfortable with the situation, so Daphne supposed everything was as it should be. But she couldn't help feeling sorry for Gloria. It was quite obvious the most pain she'd ever had to endure was the tightening of her orthodontic braces when she was a teenager.

"I don't think I could stand knowing you suffered like that." Alex looked pale.

"Well, at least Beatrice has decided to stay away." Daphne gave him a reassuring smile. "Somehow I think Gloria and Phillip are better off doing this by themselves."

"I agree. But I'll keep matters in hand until you return." Alex gave her a swift kiss on the cheek, which made Daphne feel even worse. How could she have kept him away from the birth of his own children?

AT FOUR-THIRTY that afternoon, Gloria's baby still hadn't arrived. Alex decided to go to the house to shower and change. There wasn't any more he could do to help Phillip. It was going to be a long night for them. Daphne had never returned, and he wanted to check on her and his children, too.

He was so glad his children were healthy and thriving. Being on the fringe of a birthing had made him realize how lucky he was to have his three little girls.

He headed to the Way house, instinctively knowing that, in spite of what Daphne had said about moving home with him, she wouldn't have done it this afternoon. He parked next to her Suburban and went to knock on the front door.

"Howdy, Alex," Danita said. "You're just in time for supper."

At the table, Daphne sat next to her father. Another plate was set for Danita. Three babies on a blanket near Daphne's feet looked in the direction of the adult voices.

Danita shooed him toward the kitchen. "Wash up, and I'll fill you a plate."

He was starving and glad to allow himself to be led toward the table—and his wife. "How are you doing?" he asked her, with a quick kiss on her cheek as he walked by her chair.

"Fine." She didn't look at him until he sat next to her. "Do we have a baby yet?"

"Nope." Gratefully, he eyed the plate Danita set in front of him. "Thank you, Danita. It looks wonderful. Cos, your wife's a wonderful cook."

"I know," Cos agreed around a mouthful of mashed potatoes. "That's why I married her."

Everyone laughed.

"Guess it's a good thing you've got your own cook

at the house, since Daphne cain't even fry an egg,'' Cos commented.

"Is that true?" Alex asked, astonished.

"It's true." Daphne barely met his gaze.

"You make beautiful artwork! How can you not be a great cook?" Alex couldn't believe this of his talented, extremely intelligent wife.

"I'm just not as much like my mother as I suppose you thought I was," she said miserably.

"Oh." Alex leaned back, perceiving at once that they were talking about completely different things. But they'd have to discuss it later, after they'd left the table and were alone. To bring a smile to Daphne's face, he nudged her with his elbow. "Hey, they gave Gloria some better drugs. Whatever she had before wasn't working. She's on an epidural thing now and seems happier, except when Beatrice showed up."

"Beatrice?" Daphne set her fork down and stared at Alex.

"Yeah, the old dragon finally popped in about the time you left."

Daphne's mental antennae quivered. "She only stayed a moment, probably."

"Actually, she stayed a couple of hours." Alex dug into the meat loaf Mrs. Way had served him. "Not that I think Phillip was all that thrilled to have her around. Gloria got so tense and crazed while she was there they decided to try an alternative type of medication. It's sad the kind of trouble Beatrice can kick up."

The phone rang, and Danita went to the kitchen to answer it. "Alex! Telephone!" Danita called.

"Excuse me." He put down his napkin, gave Daphne's hand a brief squeeze and got up to take the call.

"What?" Alex demanded a moment later, his voice carrying in from the kitchen.

Daphne's insides knotted.

Something was wrong.

ALEX STARED at his wife as she walked into the small, sunflower-painted kitchen. "Are you positive?" he said into the receiver. But he was staring at Daphne.

She looked at him worriedly. *Please don't let anything have happened to the baby!* was all she could think.

"Thank you," Alex said, slowly hanging up the phone. After a moment, he stiffly turned to stare at Daphne.

"That was a call Sinclair forwarded to me here," he began. "It was your uncle Herman."

"Uncle Herman?" *Not the hospital, at least.*

"Yes. Apparently, he's wondering about the payment he was promised of several thousand dollars for the steers."

"Oh," Daphne murmured, trying to imagine that much money. She had a crumpled twenty-dollar bill in her purse left over from her last stained-glass showing—and maybe one hundred dollars in the personal checking account she'd had before she married Alex. He'd given her an account in her name when they'd married, but she'd never needed to write anything against it. Up until the time she'd quit working, she had been able to pay for everything with her own income—and proud of it. They hadn't been married very long before she'd found herself pregnant…and then she'd left. It hadn't seemed right to touch any of the money after that.

"Why didn't he call Beatrice?" Daphne asked, deciding that looking too far into the past wasn't healthy for her.

He sighed. "I don't know. He says he's tried calling her numerous times, but she hasn't returned his calls."

"Maybe she's at the hospital."

Alex shrugged. "Could be. I'm going to talk to her. I want to know what's going on. She made an agreement with your uncle, and she needs to pay him. Even if she did let her cattle take off."

A cold knot hit Daphne's stomach, a strange premonition she couldn't identify. All she could think of as she stared into the face of her kind, trusting husband was that, knowing Beatrice, matters were about to take a turn for the worse.

TWO HOURS LATER, Daphne still hadn't heard from Alex. She'd cleaned up the dinner dishes, bathed the babies, fed them and put them to bed. She wanted to call the hospital and check on Gloria, but in light of Alex's comment that Gloria had been upset with Beatrice's intrusion, she decided against calling. She had wanted peace and quiet during her delivery, and Gloria no doubt felt the same.

Of course, Daphne had also wanted Alex there with her and had been too proud to call.

That was the single biggest regret of her life. It was eating a hole in her emotions. Watching Phillip and Gloria share the surprise and anticipation of their delivery had brought home to Daphne exactly what she'd done. She had tried to tell Alex at the hospital that she was sorry, but he'd had his mind on Phillip and Gloria and hadn't really paid attention.

Of course, how did she apologize for stealing something so important from him? Especially when she was supposed to love Alex too much to cause him pain? Now that she knew the full magic of the childbirthing process—and knew that she wouldn't be able to do it again—she knew what she'd taken from him.

It wasn't good enough to say she'd been frightened by his promise to his father, that she'd been terrified of letting him down, absolutely turned inside out by the thought of disappointing him when she already felt inadequate.

The truth was, he'd married down when he asked her to be his wife. Hearing Alexander say that he'd chosen Daphne for Alex had pushed her over the edge of normal emotional reasoning.

Now she was having to deal with the results of her cowardice. Would she ever stop being a minus in their marriage?

"Daphne."

Danita's voice interrupted her disconcerted musings. "Yes, Mother?"

"We can watch the babies if you want to go up to the mansion."

Daphne hesitated. "Are you sure you don't mind?"

Danita shrugged, glancing over her shoulder at Cos. He sat in his favorite chair, reading the newspaper, totally oblivious to anything going on around him. "We've got no big plans."

"Thanks, Mom." Daphne leaned down to kiss her. "To be honest, I'd like to have a chance to speak to Alex alone."

"Thought so. Been a while since you had that chance with no babies and no in-laws. 'Course, Beatrice'll probably want to start an argument while you're there, but you don't let her. Just go up to Alex's room and lock the door, for heaven's sake." She pushed a lock of hair away from Daphne's eyes. "Get it all outta your system, gal."

Daphne tried to smile, but it was hard. "I'll try."

A moment later, after she'd brushed her hair and made herself more presentable, she dashed out the door, jumped into her Chevy and swiftly drove up the road.

At Green Forks, a surprised Sinclair let her in the house when she rang the bell. "Alex is upstairs," he told her.

"Thanks." Daphne hurried up the staircase, which had yet to be repapered in the gold Beatrice wanted, though the Banning boors were still not in their customary places. "Alex!" she called, walking to his office.

He turned, looking so stern she was instantly worried. "Are you all right?"

"I'm fine. I should be better, I suppose, since Beatrice has apparently gone back to Philly."

"Philly?" Daphne repeated, a cramp stabbing her stomach like a wintry wind. "She didn't stay to see her son's baby?"

"Oh, she went by the hospital again on her way out of town. Just long enough to look at her new granddaughter, I imagine."

"Is Gloria all right?"

"Yes. When Phillip called to tell me, he sounded none the worse for wear, either."

"I'm glad." Daphne felt an immediate bonding with Gloria. Being a mother was a wonderful thing. What he'd said registered on her suddenly. "Didn't they tell us they were expecting a boy?"

"Apparently sonograms can be read incorrectly even in the big city." Alex walked to the window to stare at the pasture. "It wouldn't have mattered what the sex was, though. Apparently, Beatrice was never worried about that."

"I thought the entailment thing hinged on male heirs." Daphne was confused, but it was the look in Alex's eyes that confused her the most. Instead of being glad Beatrice was gone—she thought he'd be jumping for joy—he appeared tired. Instead of being happy about Phillip and Gloria having a girl he seemed unconcerned, except for the momentary smile when he'd mentioned the proud parents were fine.

"As I'd said before, entailment in America isn't recognized, no matter how much Dad was living with his roots in his British ancestry." Alex still didn't look her way. "There was only one heir to Dad's estate—me."

"Is that why Beatrice left?"

"I don't think so." Alex was quiet. "She left because my lawyer filed a countersuit against her, contesting her claim to Green Forks."

"I see." Daphne didn't, but with her husband so weary, she chose not to concentrate on legal matters. "Alex, there's something I don't understand. Why did Alexander never tell you about his sister?"

"Bad blood, easy enough to understand with Beatrice." He ran a hand absently through his hair before looking at her. "My mind's been so occupied ever since Dad died," he said, almost to himself. "I would never have remembered the safe if Joshua hadn't found a copy of the divorce papers."

"Alex—" Daphne began.

He shook his head. "I had put them in the personal safe in my room, which made me recall that Dad had a safe, too. No one has the combination except the lawyer, so I had a hunch it contained important papers. I called Joshua, and he dug up the combination. What do you suppose I found when I opened it?"

"I don't know," Daphne murmured.

"Documents in which Beatrice agreed to sell her portion of Green Forks to Dad. She didn't want anything to do with it—or him—and she says so in a letter." He gave her a grim smile. "Although apparently my aunt has overextended herself financially in Philly, which my new, hardworking lawyer was able to discover. When he had called to tell her my father had passed away, she quickly realized he didn't have any idea she wasn't entitled to anything. Thinking she could come down here and make a quick buck somehow, she hopped the first plane she could catch. Hence the fast attempt at an estate auction and the immediate cattle purchase. She didn't expect her moneymaking project to run off on her."

It should have been funny, but there was no amusement in Alex's tone. "She certainly did work fast. I still don't understand why Alexander didn't warn you she might come and try to finagle something out of his estate."

"According to Sinclair, Dad's old lawyer had done the paperwork to buy out Beatrice's portion many years ago. He and Beatrice had never exchanged so much as a Christmas card in the last twenty years. Unfortunately, the new lawyer was so green he knew nothing about the situation."

"But Sinclair?" Daphne allowed her gaze to rest on Alex, searching his features.

"Sinclair knew of Beatrice, knew she and Dad had come to an agreement, but he wasn't in Dad's confidence as to the entire matter. And there toward the end, Dad was rambling so much about heirs and kingdoms that Sinclair wasn't reading Dad's real concern. I have to confess I wasn't, either. I humored him every time he brought up male heirs."

"Is there anything I can say? Do?"

"No." He ran a hand through his hair. "As far as I know at this moment, I'm on the hook for paying for the cattle Beatrice bought."

"*What?*"

He chewed the inside of his jaw for a moment before answering. "Joshua says that if I had the cattle, I could return them, but the cost of getting them out here had to have been prohibitive. My only choice is to sell the ones that have been found, not that they'll get a good price in this market, as your uncle Herman very well knew."

"Oh, no." Daphne's blood began racing.

"And though I could sue Beatrice for sticking Green Forks with the bill, it likely wouldn't do me any good. She has no money, and another lawsuit would just end up costing me more." He shook his head, his expression wry. "Maybe I could press Phillip into indentured servitude. That sounds feudal enough to suit Dad, doesn't it?"

"I'm so sorry. I don't know what else to say."

He looked at her, his eyes flat and weary. "I can't help thinking that we should have known each other well enough to get through some difficult times, Daph. We should have been able to lean on each other instead of pulling apart."

He turned his head so he wasn't looking at her. Daphne was aware that his mind wasn't focused on her. That was so unlike him and so startling that she felt suddenly anchorless.

"If you don't mind, Daphne, I think I'll turn in. I've got a lot on my mind."

"Oh." Daphne bowed her head. "I've made a mess of everything."

"Well, we had a lot of help." Alex crossed his arms, his face impassive and cool as he looked at her. "But I don't want to think anymore about it tonight. I just want to…be alone so I can think this through."

Dimly, Daphne realized she had been dismissed. There wasn't anything she could say to help her husband, after all.

"Okay. I'll see you later." She felt terrible saying that! She shouldn't be leaving her husband when he was so down! But she'd left him in the first place, and then she'd left him again, so was it any wonder he didn't want her now?

Miserable with the pain of her husband's sudden reserve, Daphne silently left the room. She knew they were right back where they'd started before Alexander died. She'd overheard a conversation and she had left Green Forks because she believed Alex didn't love her.

Now she was leaving Green Forks—and this time, she could be certain his feelings for her had changed. He had always done everything he could to be with her, whether climbing ladders in the night or sitting up at any hour helping her feed and comfort their babies.

Her heart shattered. Alex didn't even want her around.

Chapter Sixteen

Alex waited until he heard Daphne's footsteps retreating before allowing his head to fall forward in a tired slump. He was exhausted in a way he had never been before, not even when he was helping take care of his three newborn daughters.

It was those damn divorce papers that were bothering him. When Joshua had called to inquire as to the status of his divorce, embarrassment had washed over Alex. He had forgotten he'd sent a copy of them to the old lawyer. For some reason, hearing Joshua, in his eager-beaver lawyer's voice, ask about his divorce had made it sound so real.

Alex didn't want it to be real, so he'd pushed the whole thing out of his mind. Joshua, naturally, was thinking about how a divorce would affect the financial position of Green Forks, something he was very right to be concerned about with Beatrice's attack on the ranch.

He hadn't known what to say. He'd mumbled, ''I'll have to get back to you later,'' and hung up the phone. But all the energy had been sucked right out of his being. He had never looked at the papers beyond an initial cursory glance. He'd been too astounded, too afraid to read the cold legalese. Wishing for a good, hot fire in the fireplace, he'd tossed the papers out of sight where he couldn't see them. Wouldn't be reminded of them.

And now he was on the hook for paying Daphne's uncle a tremendous sum of money. Unfortunately, the ranch would have to absorb the drain. When he could think again, he would sit down and decide what changes would have to be made to meet this crisis. But it had been discouraging, to say the least, to tell Joshua the woman who had filed for a divorce from him was related to the man he found himself owing money to.

He liked Joshua. Obviously the man was going to be an excellent attorney. He was just too good at turning over stones in his eagerness to prove himself to Alex.

Alex didn't want to look under any stones right now. He wanted a lot of things to stay hidden away where he wouldn't have to deal with them until he felt more prepared.

Rubbing his eyes, he sank into a chair, sighing. "I miss you, Dad," he murmured. With Beatrice's uninvited arrival, he hadn't had time to grieve for his father, nor enjoy his own new fatherhood.

There was no getting that lost time back. "I could use your advice, Dad," he said out loud. "You were such a pillar. I don't think I ever realized how firmly you were keeping me on stable ground."

Silence met his musing. He thought about Daphne, how her face had pinched with dismay when she realized he'd gotten stuck with Beatrice's bill. Daphne didn't know the magnitude of the problem. As much as Green Forks was worth, he didn't have the ready cash to pay for the cattle Beatrice had bought. His father's estate had inheritance taxes that had to be paid, a hefty sum by itself. The cattle, vanished as they were, would exhaust the food stores he'd purchased for his stock—if and when the cowboys could round up enough of the beasts for him to sell them at a loss.

It had seemed so much easier when his father was alive. "I miss you shouting," he said to his father. "You'd be on the phone yelling right now, and people would be running to do what you wanted. You'd have this problem fixed right away."

"Sir?" Sinclair poked his head around the doorway.

"Sinclair," Alex sighed, "don't call me sir. It makes me feel old. And I feel enough that way as it is."

"Would you like dinner in your room?"

Alex realized he hadn't eaten. "Thank you, Sinclair. That would be nice."

"Quiet around here, isn't it?" Sinclair entered with the tray, having anticipated Alex's appetite.

"Yes. Thankfully."

"Glad to see the back of your aunt, I must say." Sinclair set the tray in front of Alex. "Anything else I can get you?"

"No. Thanks."

Sinclair left the room, leaving Alex to ponder what he would like if someone could get it for him. A wife who hadn't filed for a divorce from him. That's what he wanted more than anything. The pain he was desperately trying to shut out of his mind rolled over him again. He lost his appetite.

He picked up the phone, dialed the hospital and asked for Gloria's room. When Phillip answered, he said, "How are the proud parents?"

"Excited. She's perfect," Phillip answered joyfully.

Alex gave a quiet, wry snort. "Aren't all babies?"

"I meant Gloria," Phillip informed him. "She did such a great job. I really appreciate you and Daphne hanging around. Gloria had a much easier time knowing she was among family."

Alex felt strange. Family? Of course that's what they were. Why else was he placing this call? Not out of a misplaced sense of pity, but because Phillip was his cousin.

"Thanks for the fruit basket," Phillip said, "and the present for Gloria. She's eaten half the fruit, and she loves the baby clothes. We were expecting a boy, you know," he confided, "but I sure do like pink. There's this one little outfit, it's got cows all over it, and even though Gloria hates cows now after that one incident at your ranch, it's her favorite. Crazy, huh?"

Alex smiled wryly at Phillip's rambling. "The whole baby thing is crazy. I'll be down in the morning to visit, if you think you'll be ready for visitors."

"That would be great. Since Mom had to get back, we're kind of…on our own."

He'd never known that feeling. Daphne's family, loony as they were sometimes, kept him surrounded with love and affection. He heard the nervousness in his cousin's voice and realized he had blessings to count, even if his father had never counted old Cos a blessing in his lifetime. "Hey, no problem. I'll be there tomorrow."

"Thanks. And thanks for the stuff, too."

"You're welcome." Alex hung up the phone, and instantly dialed Daphne's number. When she answered, he took a deep breath to slow the pounding of his heart. "Daphne?"

"Yes, Alex?"

"Phillip and Gloria are very much enjoying a fruit basket, a gift of something for Gloria I didn't quite catch—"

"Perfume," Daphne supplied. "And one of my stained-glass frames."

"Ah. And also a few baby outfits, one she likes most particularly because it has little cows on it."

"Oh, yeah. That was the cutest thing I ever saw."

Alex tapped the desktop indecisively. "So we sent a bunch of gifts over to them."

"Yes, we did. I knew you would want that."

"You're right. Thanks." Alex took a deep breath. "Daphne?"

"Yes?"

"I'm sorry I was short with you earlier."

There was no answer for a moment. Then she said, "I understand, Alex. I really do. I'm sorry my dad was the one who suggested Uncle Herman call Beatrice about his livestock."

She didn't get it. Yes, he was upset about money, but he was more upset that she hadn't come back to him when he needed her so much. Danita had said to let Daphne be the stubborn one. Sinclair and Nelly had hinted that Alex was too domineering with Daphne. But it wasn't about money. It never had been.

He wasn't about to beg. If she wasn't going to move back where she belonged, into this house so they could work on their marriage and be a family, then so be it.

"Good night, Daphne," he murmured. "I appreciate you sending gifts to Phillip and Gloria."

He barely waited for her reply before he hung up the phone. He stared out the window at the pasture, darkly dotted by moving shapes in the night as the cows moved among the hay bales. What he'd wanted to say to his wife was, *It's time for you and the children to come home. There's no Beatrice, no entailment, no reason for us not to work out the problems we've caused between us. I've been patient, damn it. I've tried to be understanding about hormones and baby blues and a multitude of other things. As bad as this may sound, I've run clean out of understanding and patience. For the sake of our children, it's time we get to work on our marriage.*

But he couldn't. Daphne had to come to him on her own.

Or else he would never know she would stay with him for always, through thick and thin, bad and good.

For better or worse.

WHEN THE DOORBELL RANG early the next morning, Alex's heart jumped. It more than jumped—it began a hammering of thrilled anticipation. Daphne had returned, he just knew it. *Be calm, he told himself, she's probably just bringing the babies for a visit.*

Sinclair walked into the den five minutes later. "Mr. Way to see you, sir," he said, imperiously showing Cos into the room.

"Thank you, Sinclair," he said, "and don't call me sir," he added softly for his employee's ears alone.

"I apologize, Alex," Sinclair said, drawing himself up. "It is my habit."

"Ah." Alex bowed his head before he went to shake his father-in-law's hand.

"Alex, I've got me an idea," Cos said heartily.

Oh, no. Alex clenched his teeth so he wouldn't say the words out loud. "Sit down and tell me about it." He forced the words out. It wasn't that he didn't like Cos—quite the contrary. But he had become quite wary of the older man and his moneymaking schemes.

"Me and you oughta go into business together," Cos said enthusiastically.

Alex raised his eyebrows as he waited for the punch line. Surely Cos wasn't serious. When his father-in-law waited for a response, he opened his eyes wide in question. "Did you have something in mind?"

"I do. We may as well combine some of our lands and do some livestock breeding, et cetera, et cetera."

"I don't know, Cos—"

Daphne's father raised a hand to stall his words. "I know what you're thinking. I'm a farmer, not a rancher. You're thinking I don't know spit about breeding. You'd be right, Alex, you'd sure be right.''

Alex tried to smile. He settled for a rather grim flex of his lips. "I thought I would be."

"But now, those Chileans have been by to see me."

"They have?" In all the Beatrice excitement, he'd forgotten about his father's bequest to Cos.

"They have, Alex, and I'm telling ya, there's gold in them four-legged critters.''

"I'm glad to hear that."

"Now, don't pawn me off with that lifted brow of yours. I got a plan." Cos leaned forward. "I got you into a bad job with the cattle Brother Herman sold your aunt. Now, who woulda figured that a Banning wouldn't have been good for the money, I ask you? We—er, Herman—sold her those cows in plumb good faith. But seeing as how you're owing Brother Herman, I say you let me pay him for them with the money the Chileans have given me for breeding my skinny cattle.''

"I can pay your brother what I owe him, Cos," Alex said stiffly. "I do appreciate you trying to help me out, though."

"No, no." Cos waved his hand airily. "Don't be saying no just yet. Your daddy already paid me once for those cows 'fore he kicked off and give 'em back to me. So it's nothing off of me to pay Brother Herman. But I've been wanting to get into business with you for a while."

"You have?" Alex couldn't digest that. Being in

business with Cos might be as dangerous as being in business with Beatrice.

"Oh, sure. What, I'm crazy, you think? We got stuff in common. A merger is obvious."

Alex leaned back in the leather chair. "What do we have in common?"

"Daphne, of course! And those sweet babies, which are living in my house."

Something in that last part snared Alex's attention. It had never bothered Cos and Danita before to have a houseful of their offspring. What was he up to?

"You see, we're family. Family's a funny thing. It's kinda like your nose. You just cain't get away from it. I mean, it's in your face. So you gotta learn to live with it."

"I—yeah. You have a point, Cos," Alex agreed, totally lost.

"And so I figure there's some profit to be made for both of us if we're in business together. You get your cattle bill paid for, and I get to go after more of this bull sperm business. I'll need a bit more land for the operation I'm considering, you see."

Alex nodded. He had a ton more land than Cos did, so he could finally see what the wiry farmer was after. "I'd get your name on the business, which will draw customer interest, and you'd get my business savor fairy, and you could use a bit of that, Alex. You know you could."

Cos's savoir faire was debatable, although Alex had to admit the old man could cook up some business. His mind was always working on a new project.

"And the biggest plus of all," Cos said on a loud

whisper, as if anyone might be in the enormous den to hear him, "is that you cain't get away from your family. Hard to ignore 'em if there's no gully between them." He looked very satisfied with his plan. "You'd get your wife back, and I'd get my house back."

Alex stared at his father-in-law incredulously. "Are you suggesting that I go into business with you so that we'll be so connected there's no point in Daphne living with you, so she might as well live with me?"

"Well, is there? I mean, if *me casa* is *su casa,* she might as well be in *su casa* as opposed to mine."

"Why don't you just ask her to move out?"

"No, I ain't kicking out my only girl." Cos shook his head. "I'm just giving her a little less motivation to feel like our house is a perteckted reserve where she can hide."

Alex frowned. "This is a rather elaborate scheme, Cos."

"All my schemes are elaborate," he confided. "When they look simple is when you realize the true greatness involved. Alexander never figured out that I was working him like a dog all those years. But I was, ya know."

"I long suspected that was the case," Alex admitted. "I even suggested as much to Daphne."

"You did?" Cos drew himself up, insulted. "What did she say?"

"She much preferred to see you as the poor serf my father was bullying."

Cos grinned bigger than a hinged teapot top. "That's my girl, always looking out for her dad. Your father wouldn't have been such an easy mark," he said with a shake of his finger, "if he hadn't really thought he was a king."

"He did that." Alex clasped his fingers over his chest. "But I can't go into business knowing I can't trust my partner."

"Trust? Why cain't you trust me?"

He shook his head at Cos's indignant squawk. "You just admitted you were cheating my father all along."

"Yeah, but he was no family of mine," Cos said with vigor. "Me and you's relations. And as I've been trying to tell ya—"

"It's like the nose on your face. You can't get away from it," Alex interrupted.

"Right. Good to see you pay attention, Alex."

He sighed heavily. "I appreciate the offer, Cos, and don't think I don't see what you're up to." Taking a second to think over his words so he wouldn't offend his father-in-law, he said, "It's just that I don't want Daphne to come home to me just because she feels like she might as well because she can't get away from me. I want her to come home because she wants to. I've had all the manipulating, game-playing machinations I can stand, whether my father's or Beatrice's or even this admittedly unique plan of yours." He made his voice soft so Cos would know he wasn't trying to dismiss the thought he'd put into his strategy. "And to be honest, I would appreciate it if you and Danita wouldn't get in the middle. I'm very serious about Daphne coming home once and for all."

"I unnerstand," Cos said quietly, "it's just I don't

think you realize, Alex, that my daughter's got herself up a tree. And she's not sure how to come down."

Alex shrugged. "All the same, while I thank you for trying to save me from paying what I owe your brother, I believe you'd have to agree that Daphne's going to have to figure a way down out of that tree this time without anyone rushing in to save her."

Cos was quiet for a few moments. Then he nodded. "All right, Alex. Rats." He smacked his lips in resignation. "I sure was looking forward to going into the breeding business, though. I need me a good, recognizable name on my business cards. Banning Breeding, I was thinking."

"No, Cos," Alex said with a laugh. "Way Breeding would be much more likely to attract attention. You do have seven children."

"Your name, my cattle," Cos insisted.

"I'll think about it," Alex said as he walked his father-in-law to the door. "Maybe if Daphne and I ever work things out, we can talk."

"Daphne coming home is the same thing as waiting on the cows to come home," Cos warned him.

"Trust me, nobody knows that better than me." Alex closed the front door after Cos had left. The likelihood of his wife or his lost cows coming home was about the same. He wouldn't bet the ranch on it.

Chapter Seventeen

"Daphne, can we talk to you for a minute?" Danita called.

Daphne put Alexis Abigail in her crib and kissed her good-night. Then she went down the hall. Cos and Danita were sitting in the den, ostensibly watching TV.

"You wanted me, Momma?" Daphne asked.

Her parents turned to look at her at the same time. "Sit down, honey. We want to talk to you."

She sat, a strange foreboding coming over her. "Yes?"

"Daphne, are you proud of us?" Danita bluntly asked.

"Yes! Of course I am!" Daphne cried. She clasped her hand to her chest. "How can you ask such a question?"

"Because we wondered, gal." Cos looked her straight in the eye. "How come you're slinking around here, acting like you ain't good enough for that boy up there? You ashamed of being a Way?"

"No! It isn't that at all!" Daphne stared at her parents in shock. "You know I'm proud of you."

Danita shook her head. "You're not acting like it."

She couldn't stand it. Folding to her knees, she clasped her parents to her. "I am so very proud of you both. You're spunky and hardworking and loyal. And you take such wonderful care of me."

"Well, we wondered." Danita ran a hand through Daphne's hair. "You used to be spunky and hard-working, too. Frankly, we're worried about you, hon."

"I've been thinking about that," she replied softly. "I know I've been different lately."

"Nope." Cos put a gnarly hand against her cheek to stroke it. "Quite frankly, you're acting like a scaredy-cat."

"I feel that way for some reason." Gently, Daphne disentangled herself from the loving hands and got into her chair. "I talked to the doctor about the fact that I'm tired all the time and that my nerves seem a bit frayed."

"And?" Danita asked.

"Well, she says I'm perfectly normal for a woman who's just a month or more past childbirth."

"Yep," Danita agreed. "And you had three young 'uns. Plus, when you shoulda been resting, you've been fretting."

"It has been unusually stressful, I suppose." Daphne gave a small shrug and smiled at her parents so they would see she still had some spirit left in her. "I felt a lot better after hearing from my doctor that I was normal and just suffering average new mom stuff. I've had some deep baby blues, but that seems to be working through my system, as well." She blew out a breath that was really a heartfelt sigh. "Tell you the truth, I have felt better every day. Stronger."

"Then how come you're so sad?" Cos demanded.

"I'm not sad," Daphne denied. But she wouldn't meet her parents' eyes.

"Daphne," Danita said softly, "we're proud of you being brave. But you don't have to be that way with us. We understood why you left him in the first place, hon, but he's done plenty to make amends. And he's hurting, too."

"I know." Her lips twisted with sadness. "It's just that things keep happening that make me feel less equal to Alex. I'm so afraid that one day he's going to look at me and think, now why did I marry that woman? Even though I know it's not rational, it's the way I feel."

"Why do you think Alex would have doubts?" Cos asked.

"Because I do," Daphne whispered. "And because I think he deserved better."

"So you are ashamed of us." Cos stood abruptly. "Daphne Way, I've been married to your mama for more years than I can count, and I've never been more proud of her than when she agreed to be my bride. It didn't matter that she was always going to be the brains in the family. It didn't matter that I was always going to let her be the boss. I might not have ever brought home the money other men did, but I love your mama with all my heart. And that, my girl, is all that counts." He gestured toward the Banning mansion. "And either you give that same love to Alex or you just let him go. Because that man ain't happy, and he already had enough to suffer over. If he was a dog, I'd say shoot him and put him out of his misery.''

''Dad!'' Daphne exclaimed.

''Well, hellfire,'' Cos complained, falling into his recliner. ''What I'm saying is make up your mind, make it up tonight and get off the fence you're straddling. All this going back and forth is wearing out my easygoing nature.'' He wrinkled his lips, exhausted from his speech.

''I know you're right.'' Daphne rose and kissed them each on the cheek. ''It's not fair to Alex. I'll tell him tonight.'' She left the room, her heart stinging from the knowledge of what she had to do.

Cos looked into Danita's eyes after Daphne was out of earshot. ''Did I overdo it?''

Danita thought for a moment. ''I'm not sure. You may have gone a bit overboard with the dead dog business.''

''Heck. I plumb lost my train of thought for some reason and started thinking about my old hunting dog.'' Cos inhaled a deep breath. ''Deer season's coming, and—''

''Cos!''

''Sorry. As I said, I got to thinking about my dog. It's his eyes! Alex is wearing that same sad look on his face that my dog gets when he can't ride in the truck.''

''I think it's far more serious than that.'' Danita glanced down the hall. ''Sh! I think I hear her coming.''

They glued their attention to the TV set.

Daphne came to stand in front of them. "Thanks, Mom and Dad. I appreciate your pep talk."

"You're a good daughter," Cos told her.

"I try. Do you mind watching the babies for a while?" Daphne asked.

"Nope. Be a pleasure." Danita gave her a soft smile. "Going somewhere?"

"I'm going to tell Alex what I think needs to be done about our marriage."

"Oh?" Cos perked up, but Danita elbowed him.

"Take your time. We're just going to sit here and watch an old movie."

"I'll be right back." Daphne left the room. They heard the front door slam. A second later the Suburban roared to life.

"Well? What do you think she's going to tell him?" Cos asked his wife.

"She's going to tell him it's over," Danita said, her eyes sad.

"How do you know?" Cos demanded.

"Because she's not spending the night. If she was telling him she was going back to him, she'da asked us to watch the babies overnight."

Cos shook his head, putting his hand over Danita's. "I guess I did overdo it," he said glumly.

"No." Danita leaned back, putting her head against the recliner cushion. "Daphne's been determined to find the escape hatch in that marriage ever since she heard Alexander babbling about boy heirs. The old coot didn't know it, but he put a curse on that marriage that can't be lifted."

There was nothing to say to that, so the two of them

sat in the dark watching TV, their hearts deeply saddened that they couldn't do anything to help their only daughter be as happy as they'd always been.

ON HER WAY up the road, Daphne wondered why she just didn't call Alex to tell him what she already knew she was going to say. But that was the cowardly way out. Their eyes needed to meet so that he could see how important what she was going to ask was to her. It was going to be the most heart-wrenching thing that had ever happened to her if Alex said no.

To her surprise, the mansion was dark. There wasn't even a porch light on. Amazed, she glanced at her watch. It was almost eleven o'clock! Daphne couldn't believe the evening had passed so quickly, but the babies had been fussier than usual.

Maybe they miss their dad.

But that was silly. They didn't really even know Alex.

They should, the voice nagged. It was true, Daphne thought as she looked at the huge mansion. They had a lot to be proud of in their father.

Cos said she was ashamed of him and Danita. Daphne lowered her gaze. She hadn't been totally honest with her folks. She wasn't ashamed of them, but the Uncle Herman cattle deal had been the icing on the cake. The marriage wasn't equal. Her side was always going to need something from Alex's side. As long as one side was constantly being asked to give, the other side was only taking. That's the way it had been forever between the two farms, and her dream marriage to Alex hadn't changed a thing.

It had gotten worse almost immediately.

That's why she had to tell him the truth tonight. She had no intention of taking another thing from him unless he understood her need to be on the giving end for a change.

Squinting at the house, Daphne pondered ringing the bell. But that would bring Nelly or Sinclair to the door, and no doubt they were sleeping.

She could go home and call Alex to warn him she was coming so he could meet her at the front door.

Or, a teasing voice suggested, she could give Alex a little bit of his own preferred method of entering her bedroom. Where that idea came from, Daphne never considered. She turned the Suburban, went to her house and loaded the ladder into the back.

Then she returned to the Banning mansion, parked and set the ladder under Alex's window.

"Just right," she muttered. "No doubt I'll fall and break my arm, but…here goes nothing." She ascended carefully and peered through the glass before tapping lightly.

Nothing happened. She'd prepared herself for Alex to appear in the window, but he wasn't there. Maybe he was downstairs watching TV. Daphne frowned. What did her husband do at night when she wasn't with him?

"Looking for something?" Alex inquired from below her.

"Aieeyyy!" Daphne shrieked.

"Be careful, Daphne!"

She didn't need the warning. Her hands were

clenched around the ladder like claws. "You startled me!"

"Now, Daph, don't act all innocent." He grinned at her, obviously glad to have gotten the upper hand. "You were going to try to sneak up on me, and I just sneaked up on you better."

"Well, that wasn't fair!" She glared at him. "I could have fallen."

"You shouldn't have been up there anyway. What if I hadn't been home? You would have wasted all this effort and maybe broken your neck."

"I was perfectly safe until you deliberately sabotaged my efforts!" she snapped.

Alex jammed his hands in his jeans pockets and looked at her thoughtfully. "Strange, but it occurs to me that we sound like your dad and my dad bickering."

She frowned at that. "What do you mean?" One by one, she began to descend the rungs.

Alex held the ladder steady. "You were trying to one-up me, and I did it to you first, so you're crying foul. Just like your father. And I'm acting like my father trying to make sure I—"

"Never mind." Daphne avoided his grasp and hopped off the ladder. "I get your drift, and it's annoying."

"What is?"

"That we so easily fall into the old pattern." She met his gaze, her head cocked. "You cannot always be king in this relationship."

"And you cannot always be the sly serf, a role Cos played to the hilt."

Daphne held in her laugh and pretended to be indignant instead. "My father is hardly sly."

"Trust me, Daph, your dad coined the word and wrote the book on it."

"I beg to differ, but there's no winning with you." Daphne picked up the ladder and started to carry it to the Chevy. After a moment, she realized Alex wasn't following. Slightly perturbed that he hadn't offered to carry the ladder, she glanced over her shoulder.

He was staring at her. And that was disconcerting, too. "What are you doing?" she demanded huffily.

"I'm letting you win. You want to take your ladder and run off. I'm letting you."

"I see." She loaded the object of debate into the van. Then she walked to the porch and waited.

"What are you doing?" Alex asked.

"Letting you win," she told him.

"How?"

She gave him a sly smile, her daddy's at its best. "You've been wanting to get me upstairs for some time now. I may let you."

"Really." Alex walked forward briskly. "I may let *you* win, in that case."

"How?" That didn't set well with Daphne. She was letting *him* win.

"By taking you there." He scooped her into his arms and said, "Don't say another word, Daphne Way Banning," before slanting his mouth over hers for a deep kiss.

"For a sore loser, you kiss pretty good," she commented a moment later, when they'd parted to take some necessary breaths.

"For a woman who wants an easy victory, you never know when to be quiet." He carried her up the stairs.

"I have a lot to say." She snuggled against his neck.

"Daphne, there's nothing I want to hear until the morning comes."

"You may regret it," she said on a teasing note.

"I can live with that kind of regret." He put her gently on the bed and joined her, smoothing her hair from her face. "I was hoping you'd come back tonight. I saw you turn your car around, and it had me worried."

That caught her attention. "You knew I'd been here?" Daphne was indignant. The element of surprise had been so crucial to her plan.

"Your father called to ask me to look out for you since it was so dark."

"Oh, for heaven's sake," Daphne said, laughing. "My parents mean well, I'm sure."

"They do. Cos wanted to make sure you made it from the truck to the porch safely. There's a lot of stray cattle running around out there, you know. My heart sank when it looked like you'd changed your mind. I was actually looking forward to being ambushed."

"Maybe I should change my mind," Daphne whispered, as he kissed each and every one of her fingertips, starting a slow, aroused burn inside her.

"Too late. I've got you here, and you're staying the night." His lips moved from her fingertips along her upper arms. "Your mother said if I could talk you into staying, she'd watch the babies."

"Wait a minute!" Daphne cried, trying to sit. "I've been set up!"

He pushed her gently against the pillows and began undoing the buttons on her blouse. "Yes. One night alone with my beautiful wife was an opportunity I thought about passing up, but decided it would be unfair not to give her that which she was seeking."

"Alex!" Daphne grabbed his fingers as he moved toward her breast. "I came up here to tell you something important, not necessarily to…to—oh, my, that feels *heavenly*." All thoughts of putting her husband off any longer flew out of her mind as he traced tiny kisses along her stomach. "I don't want you to see my scar," she whispered, lifting his head between her palms so she could see into his eyes.

"I have never met a woman with more worries." He lowered his head, moving toward the area of her body Daphne was most concerned about her husband seeing. "I take it as my most pressing duty to alleviate your fears at once. I want the sexual lioness who was proud of her fit body back."

He placed kisses along one hip, and Daphne felt herself beginning a dangerous melt. "I'm not fit anymore."

"After a night with your husband, you'll be a lot closer to the definition. For that matter, so will I," he groaned as she traced her fingernails lightly over his back.

"Let me take your shirt off, Alex."

"I'm busy," he murmured, somewhere between the region of her navel and her panty line.

"Alex!" she protested, squirming. "You undid my blouse. Fair is fair."

"Your chest is so much prettier than mine, though." He placed a kiss against the front clasp of her bra where her blouse parted. Suddenly, he looked into her eyes. "Daphne, am I moving too fast for you?"

"Maybe a little." For some reason, she was overcome by shyness she hadn't known since the first time they'd made love.

He considered that for a moment before moving to rest against the pillow beside her and hold her in his arms. "I know just what we need," he whispered huskily.

"What?"

"We need to get to know each other all over again."

It felt so good to be in the shelter of his arms. She closed her eyes and enjoyed the sensation of being in bed with him. "It does feel kind of different than before, doesn't it?"

"Well, we're not the same people that we were before. We're parents now. You're a mother, I'm a father. That's bound to change us. You've gained some weight, I've gained some gray hair."

She giggled. "You know I should be angry that you mention my weight."

He nuzzled her neck. "Daph, I love the weight you gained. Those three little girls of ours are amazing."

"They are, aren't they? Did you notice how Danielle's looking around her more now?"

"Yes, and did you notice that Sabrina's eyelashes are starting to grow out?"

They were silent for a moment.

"Alexis Abigail is still the quietest, most peaceful child I have ever seen," Daphne said. "I've been very worried that there's something wrong with her. Do you think she sees? Hears?"

"She seems fine to me, honey. Did you ask the pediatrician what he thought?"

"He says she appears normal. That later on we can run some tests, but that right now, she's just a healthy, wonderful infant." The tenseness started to creep into Daphne's shoulders.

"What do you want her to do, Daphne? What do you think she should be doing?"

"Crying. Demanding something. Not just lying around all the time taking everything in."

He kissed his wife's shoulders to diminish the tension he sensed building. "You know, my dad loved all three of those girls. The day you brought home babies, Daphne Banning, you brought home my father's dream."

"Really?"

"Yes." Alex thought for a moment. "Not that I could accuse my father of playing favorites, but I could have sworn he and Alexis Abigail had bonded in some uncanny way. He just seemed drawn to her, and she seemed to trust him."

Sentimental tears popped into Daphne's eyes. "I know."

"Remember when you named her Abigail for 'father is rejoicing'?" He held his wife against his chest, and Daphne put her head against him, hearing his strong heartbeat. "I can honestly say that my father was rejoicing in all his grandchildren, Daph. And that you gave him happiness before he died is something I can never thank you enough for. It made his passing bearable, knowing you had given him that which he wanted more than anything."

"Not a boy, though."

He tucked her hair behind her ear absently. "He didn't care, Daph. You should have seen that for yourself when he bought those christening gowns."

"I saw it for myself when he took Alexis Abigail from the minister. I can still remember how his hands trembled as if he were holding the most special thing in the world."

"He was, honey. That was all my dad wanted. And you gave him triple his wildest hopes."

"I'm so glad." She tilted her head to look at him. "Alex?"

"Yes?"

"I'm sorry about your father. I haven't taken as good care of you as I should have since he died."

He sighed, tracing one finger along her cheek. "I didn't do some things the way I should have, either." Resting his chin on top of her head, he said, "Nothing prevents us from starting over, though."

"How do we?"

"Like this." He moved her until he was facing her. "Daphne, my wife, I haven't told you lately how much I love your hair when it turns fire-lit bronze when the sun shines on it. Don't ever cut it, even when you get old.''

She smiled. ''Please, Alex, it'll be gray then. And gray hair to my ankles won't be comfortable.''

''I meant, don't cut it off short, at least until I'm as old as Cos.''

''Okay. I agree, as long as you agree not to ever wear those elastic-waist pants with no belt loops on them when you finally develop a paunch. And no comb overs when you start losing your hair.''

''Okay.'' He ran a gentle finger over her eyebrows, which always seemed arched with curiosity. ''I want you to always look at me with happiness in those green eyes. I never want to see pain.''

She nodded. ''The same goes for your baby blues.''

''And this sloping nose, which I hope my girls got rather than mine, I want it to always stay the same.''

''Well, I'll try,'' Daphne said, laughing softly. ''Unless I fall off a ladder or something else unfortunate.'' She studied Alex's aristocratic nose. ''I do tend to think that perhaps yours might be a bit masculine for a girl.''

He cupped his hand under her chin and drew her to him for a long kiss, which she gave herself up to completely. ''Of course, it's your lips I have always found the most appealing thing about you.''

''Why?'' Her gaze lit on his as she thought about what his lips had always been able to do to her.

''They're you, Daphne Banning, kind of full, kind of easygoing, definitely sexy.''

For answer, she pressed her lips to his, taking her time. She felt him respond to her tongue as she lightly tasted his mouth. He groaned, and when he reached to undo her bra, Daphne unbuttoned his shirt—and his pants, making short work of the zipper, too. ''I forgot how much fun undressing you is.''

''I didn't forget how much I like undressing you.'' He gave a playful growl as he slid her bra off. ''I'll take my time when I get to your panties, if you don't mind.''

She could feel the rigid evidence of his desire for her through the boxers he wore. ''I'm not in much of a hurry myself.''

''Good.''

His touch thrilled her as he slid his palms over her buttocks and down the backs of her legs. Daphne sighed, scooting as close to him as she could get. With both hands, she eased his boxers off him. ''I see you've missed me,'' she said, her lips curving in a rather pleased smile.

He groaned as she took him in her hands. ''You don't have to see to know that I've missed you.'' Cupping her breasts in his palms, Alex groaned again as he ran his thumbs over the hardness of her nipples. ''Are you sure you're ready?''

''Oh, I'm definitely ready,'' she whispered, placing one of his hands so he could feel the moistness of her panties.

He slid them off her immediately. ''Oh, Daphne.'' His fingers slid back and forth along the slick curve hidden between her legs. ''I meant, does the doctor say you can…''

''Resume marital relations?'' she murmured against his belly as she kissed a trail of pleasure that had him praying the answer was yes. ''The doctor says everything is fine, just to go easy.''

Carefully, he maneuvered his wife underneath him. ''Tell me if I do anything to hurt you.''

''I will.'' She gazed up into his eyes and guided him to her.

He was as gentle as he knew how to be, slowly moving inside her. ''Are you okay?'' he asked, watching her face for signs of pain.

''I'm fine,'' she whispered. ''Don't stop now.'' Her hands pressed against his buttocks, drawing him farther inside.

''Daphne,'' he said on a moan when he'd entered her completely. Laying his head in the crook of her neck, he remained still, not moving a muscle. ''I'm so afraid of hurting you.''

She ran her fingertips along his spine. Then, taking his face between her palms, she kissed his lips, over and over again, until he understood that she wanted him to continue making love to her.

Relieved, Alex moved inside his wife, feeling her, reveling in her, enjoying her. And when she cried out her pleasure a few moments later, he closed his eyes tight, driven by the climax pressing him for release. ''Oh, Daphne,'' he groaned, allowing himself to go into the outstretched comfort of her arms.

The feeling of being with her again was heaven. Whatever it took, he would never lose her again.

Chapter Eighteen

In the morning, Alex awakened to the scent of Daphne and the feel of her wrapped in his arms. He hadn't forgotten how much he loved holding his wife, and having her here sent a profound gratitude washing over him.

"Good morning," he murmured against her neck.

She arched against him. "Mmm. I don't think I've had this much sleep since before the babies were born."

He nipped a kiss on her shoulder. "If you were getting that much sleep, then obviously I wasn't doing my job."

She giggled, opening green velvet eyes. His heart paused. He could do nothing but stare at his lovely, sleep-tousled wife.

"You did your job. I just finally relaxed. It could have been not keeping one ear open to listen for my babies," she said, one brow raised thoughtfully, "or it could have been the satisfying lovemaking my husband gave me."

A light knock on the door arrested Alex's reply, but he most certainly intended to get the answer he wanted to hear out of her. With a meaningful look her way, he called, "Yes?"

"Breakfast, sir?" Nelly's voice came through the door.

"Are you hungry?" he whispered so Nelly wouldn't hear. He wasn't sure if Daphne wanted her presence announced yet.

She nodded eagerly.

"Say it was your husband's lovemaking that brought you such good slumber," he commanded.

She grinned saucily at him. "Oh, it most definitely was."

"Yes, I would like breakfast, Nelly," he called loudly.

"I'll leave it outside your door, then."

"Thank you." Wrapping the bedspread around his midsection so he wouldn't startle anyone in the hall, he opened the door to get the tray. He brought it inside and said, "Well, I hope you weren't trying to keep your visit a secret. Nelly and Sinclair brought you breakfast, too, or else they think I'm really hungry."

Two glasses of orange juice, two plates with eggs, bacon and aromatic biscuits graced the tray, as well as a lovely rose in a crystal vase.

"Oh, how nice!" Daphne sat up. "I love being served for a change." She took a plate and a glass and began eating with gusto. "I'm glad they knew I was here and brought extra. I'd hate to have made you go without breakfast."

"You eat like your daddy." Alex smiled at her. "I

see now where Sabrina and Danielle get their appetites."

"Do they ever. I wish Alexis would eat more." Daphne paused, her eyes losing some of their sparkling pleasure.

"She will one day. She's just fine, Daph. Don't go borrowing trouble." He dug into his breakfast, too, after he'd pulled on jeans.

Daphne remembered she wanted to talk to her husband about something. "Alex?"

"Yeah?" He bit into a biscuit and waited.

"There really was a reason I came over last night." He put the biscuit down. "Yes?"

She took a deep breath. "You know I have my stained-glass artwork in a boutique in town, as well as several other places."

"Yes."

"Well, a collector from the northwest came through and saw my things. She wanted a bunch of pieces for a store she has up there. What she paid me came to about ten thousand dollars."

"That's great, Daph!" Alex couldn't believe she'd waited so long to tell him. "Didn't I tell you your work was different? Original? Fabulous?"

He had always believed in her, Daphne acknowledged silently. "I want you to take the money she paid me, Alex, and I want you to use it to pay part of what you owe Uncle Herman."

"No, Daph. I appreciate it, I do, but—"

The wistful look in her green eyes stopped him. There was something else, maybe hurt, that caught Alex's attention and made him reassess what he was saying. "I mean, the bill will be paid, honey, if that's what you're worried about."

She pushed her breakfast away. "No. I know you have plenty of money, Alex. That's what Beatrice came all the way down here for, after all."

"Well, sweetheart, then what's the problem? You don't have to give me your money. You worked hard for it."

"I know."

She crossed her arms, a gesture that brought her full breasts to prominence through the sheet she'd pulled up under her arms. He tried very hard to keep his mind on what his wife was trying to say, in spite of the splendid view.

"But you work hard, too. If we're going to be partners, we're going to be full partners. I don't want a marriage where you do all the giving." She stared at him, her heart in her throat. "I'm very serious about this, Alex. I can understand why you wouldn't want to go into business with my dad, but there's no reason you can't take a little help from your wife."

"It's not your fault the cattle ran off, Daphne. That was Beatrice's doing. I haven't talked to the insurance company, but I'm sure they'll pay a claim for animals that were delivered to—"

"I don't care about that, Alex! I care about being equal partners. And I know it's not a lot of money, that it's just a drop in the bucket compared to what you've got. But if the marriage is always going to be based on unequal footing where you never let me give anything, well, then…" Her eyelashes swept down in disappointment. "Then it's not really a marriage."

He thought about that for a few minutes. His wife felt less than equal to him. She'd said that when she'd left him. For some reason, she didn't realize she gave him so much more than he could ever give her. But it didn't really matter anymore who was right and who was wrong. If they were going to put the pattern of one-upping behind them, then it had to start now. He admired his wife for her perception and sensitivity—and her desire to make their marriage work. It was what he had wanted, after all, and if it meant doing this her way, then he would.

Suddenly, he understood what Danita had been trying to tell him. It wasn't doing everything Daphne's way. It was considering her feelings that counted most to her.

He lifted her hand to kiss it. Then he said, "Daphne, I really, really need to borrow some money to pay Uncle Herman. Do you think you could loan me some?"

A slow smile spread over her face. Her eyes lit up with happiness and pride in her accomplishment. "Why, husband," she said, "I just happen to have some you could borrow—for the rest of our lives."

ALEX'S REALIZATION of Daphne's feelings caused him to be generous in ways he would never have suspected he might be—all because his wife and their three daughters were moving under his roof the next day.

"Do you mind if I invite Phillip and Gloria to stay at Green Forks for a while?" he asked Daphne as she put away baby linens.

"I was trying to think of how I could ask you the same question."

"Really?" That startled him, considering she'd once been envious of Gloria.

"Yes. I think Phillip could learn a lot from you." She smiled luminously at her husband.

"There's a small house on the outskirts of Banning land they could move into. Nothing like what they're used to, I'm sure. But Phillip indicated some interest in learning ranching—"

"No, he didn't," Daphne said, laughing.

"I think he meant taking pictures of it, actually." Alex picked up the baby suitcases she'd packed. "Did you know my cousin is a decent photographer? He wanted to pursue a career in it, but Beatrice didn't think he should work at that menial job, as she put it. He's ready to try his hand at it."

"Good." She went to get another bag. "Gloria will need lots of sunscreen to keep her skin looking the way it does."

"Neiman Marcus is but a trip into Dallas." He eyed his wife as she competently packed. "I think she's hoping you'll show her the ropes about breast-feeding."

Daphne stopped what she was doing to stare at him. "Did she say that?"

"Yeah." He felt a blush rising up the back of his neck. "It's not going too well in the hospital. She says if you can nurse more than one, she ought to be able to breast-feed the one she's got."

"I'm so surprised. I thought she'd rather not do anything that would be…messy."

Alex grinned at her. "Surprised me, too. Maybe it's all this good Texas air causing the changes they're considering."

"Are you sure you can trust them?" Daphne couldn't help asking.

"Yeah. The estate is secure, Daphne. It goes to our three little girls without conditions."

She nodded. "I'm glad you got all that worked out. That entailment business scared me. I never want to hear that word again."

Cos and Danita came in, eyeing the last of the baby things as they were being stacked to be carried to the Chevy. Cos held out his hand. "Well, it'd be harder to get rid of my little girl if I hadn't gotten me a new business partner."

"Business partner?" Daphne asked, her eyes going straight to Alex.

"Yep. Me and Alex shook on it this morning." Cos beamed from ear to ear as Alex shook his hand again.

"Did you really?" she asked, her voice trembling with hope.

"We did." Alex nodded, delighted he'd surprised her. "I've been needing a strong, savvy business partner for a long time. This breeding business interests me, and your father is just the ticket."

"Oh, Alex!" Daphne glowed at him, her eyes promising his just reward later on when they were alone in the Banning mansion. "Congratulations to both of you."

"No," Alex said, smiling at his babies as they lay on a pallet nearby, "congratulations to all of us."

By the happy smile on his wife's face, Alex knew he'd scored big-time. He'd been more than happy to agree to Cos's plan for great gain. After all, there was plenty to be gained in this venture for both of them.

More important, he wanted to prove to Daphne that he considered her family equal to his.

And that he loved her.

Cos threw an arm around his daughter's shoulder and one around Alex's. "Let's drink on it, and to a wonderful future between the Bannings and the Ways."

"I could stand a glass of champagne," Alex agreed. His gaze held Daphne's with the promise of many wonderful years ahead of them.

"I got sumpin' better than champagne," Cos said with a grin. He took his arms down and pushed Alex and Daphne together. 'Ya'll stand right here. I'll be back in a jiff."

He was back a second later with two jelly jars full of a clear, sparkling liquid. He handed one to each of them.

Alex raised his glass, pausing when he realized Cos wasn't holding a glass. "Aren't you having any?"

Cos grinned, his face wreathed with playful delight. "Naw, I've drunk my share of that."

Alex shrugged and raised his glass to Daphne. "To a profitable future with my new business partner— and many days of happiness with my lovely wife."

"Thank you," Daphne softly replied. "Cheers."

At the same time, they drank the crystalline liquid, which shimmered with gently effervescent bubbles.

"This is delicious," Alex said, his gaze never leaving Daphne's. "It *is* better than champagne. What is it, Cos?"

The wiry old man chuckled before slapping Alex on the back and kissing his daughter on the cheek. "Well water! The secret to my success. And I'm passing it on to you."

Alex glanced at him. "Well water?"

"That's right." He leaned close to whisper, "You didn't think Danita and I had all those big, healthy boys without help, did ya? Look at me, skinny as a rail. But not my boys," he stated proudly. He nodded at Daphne. "Nor my girl."

Daphne shook her head at her father. "Dad's giving you a line of bull," she told Alex. "He's been talking about that silly well of his for years. It's just a plain old artesian well. Nothing special about it. If there was, he could have bottled it and been a millionaire by now."

Cos chuckled. As he and Danita left the room, he called, "I've been rich all my life by the only measure that counts, Daphne Way."

Her eyes glowed as Alex kissed her fingertips. "He's right, you know. His family has been his yardstick of success."

"I know." She inhaled a quick, excited breath as her husband moved closer, his eyes shining with intent. "But he makes me crazy when he talks about his magic underground well."

"You know, my father said your dad had to have some secret to getting all those male children."

"Well, he did." Daphne moved willingly into

Alex's arms. "My mother loved him with all her heart. The same way I love you."

"I love you, Daphne." He kissed her forehead before making his way down to her cheek. "Maybe we should finish our water, just in case. Your dad seems to think it does something for virility."

"Do you need help?" she asked with a provocative smile. "You never have before."

"No, but your father's such a good salesman, I'd be crazy not to trust him. We are partners now, you know."

"Then bottoms up," she said, finishing her water and putting down her glass.

Alex drained his glass and set it down, then pulled Daphne tight against him. "It's starting to work already," he told her. "I can feel it."

She giggled as his hands cupped her bottom and pressed her to him. "I can feel it, too."

"Shall we go test the cause and effect of magic well water?" he asked.

"Immediately," she agreed, slowly sliding her arms around his neck, "but I should warn you that, for the sake of accuracy, testing must be done many times to be conclusive."

"Thank heavens," he said, scooping his wife into his arms to carry her over the threshold of their temporary bedroom. "I never told you this, but I find your scientific side very appealing."

"I am an artist," she said with a laugh.

"No," he corrected, setting her on the bed and joining her, "you are a scientific, artistic, undefinable woman."

"Can you live with that?"

"I can." He kissed her neck. "And if our three little daughters grow up to be anything like you, I'll consider myself as lucky as old Cos."

"You will?" Her eyes shone.

"I will." He pulled her to him, and she gladly surrendered to his touch. "I already do. I got the woman of my dreams and three special daughters."

She sighed with happiness. "I got the man of my dreams and three special daughters."

"Is there anything else needed for a happy ending?"

"Nothing," she murmured, melting into his arms. "Nothing at all."

Epilogue

One year later, on the very date on which Alexander Senior had passed away, Alex and Daphne discovered they were expecting another child. They knew, without a doubt, that a miracle had happened and that somewhere in heaven, Alexander was, indeed, rejoicing. A son was born to them nine months later, his lusty cries so demanding that the happy parents immediately knew he would make his Banning ancestors proud.

In due time, the baby girls grew into adorable young ladies, secure in the love of their parents. Little brother was cherished by his sisters, who toted him from room to room like a favorite puppy. They cuddled and spoiled him—and let him know that, even if he was the only male child in the home, *they* ruled the roost. Which was just fine with him.

The girls came into their own with fiery independence and brilliance and made their mother proud. Danielle Constance became a rocket scientist, which amused her doting father, since Daphne had nicknamed her Yoda. Miss Magoo, or Sabrina Caroline, grew lashes of such length, and artistic ability of such renown, that she went on to create her own line of cosmetics. And tiny—some might say runty—Alexis Abigail, the ugliest baby her father had ever laid eyes on, grew up to win the Miss Universe crown before graduating magna cum laude from Harvard. It was her dream to study fertility treatments and open a practice where she could help all women who wanted to have a baby.

Alexander Junior was another matter. His early adulthood was spent in such pursuits as playing handball in Nassau and fire walking in Tibet, much to his father's dismay. There was the summer he spent selling used cars with Uncle Bob, a job he took to with amazing aptitude, even to the point of thinking about going into the family business. For his father's birthday one year, Alexander announced he had been accepted to Harvard, a monumental feat that Daphne had helped him accomplish. Alex cried tears of joy when his son graduated, smiling a little when Alexander tapped the dean on the head with the sheepskin.

After graduating from law school—and on a lark—Alexander decided to go into politics. After years of using his abilities to get along with many different personality types—a benefit of having three older, opinionated sisters—he became governor of Texas.

And so, finally, the tradition of male ancestral portraits could carry on. An oil painting of Alexander Junior, revered and respected, was hung in the great hall of Green Forks, right next to the oil paintings of Sabrina, Danielle and Alexis Abigail—and their father.

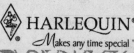

If you enjoyed what you just read,
then we've got an offer you can't resist!

Take 2 bestselling
love stories FREE!

Plus get a FREE surprise gift!

COMING NEXT MONTH

#761 SECRET DADDY by Vivian Leiber
Gowns of White
Dr. Corey Harte had wealth, success—but no special lady in his life. There had only ever been one woman: Robyn O'Halloran. It had been four years since their secret night together. Little did he know the secret she carried with her....

#762 A MAN FOR MEGAN by Darlene Scalera
The Ultimate...
Megan Kelly thought she had it all: a steady paycheck, her own house, food on the table. Then there was Gino, who had the commanding air of an Arabian aristocrat, the playfulness of a boy and the intensity of a man, who made her realize that smoldering kisses should be a major food group. But Megan could never give him her heart....

#763 LET'S MAKE A BABY! by Jacqueline Diamond
To avoid an arranged marriage, Annalisa de la Pena needed to find a willing man who would father her child. Ryder Kelly was the man she chose. But Ryder wanted more than a fling—he wanted to know what Annalisa was hiding....

#764 FOR BETTER, FOR BACHELOR by Nikki Rivers
What do you get when world-famous foreign correspondent Marcus Slade comes to the tiny town of Birch Beach, Wisconsin? Trouble! Especially when small-town girl Rachel Gale snares his heart....

Look us up on-line at: http://www.romance.net